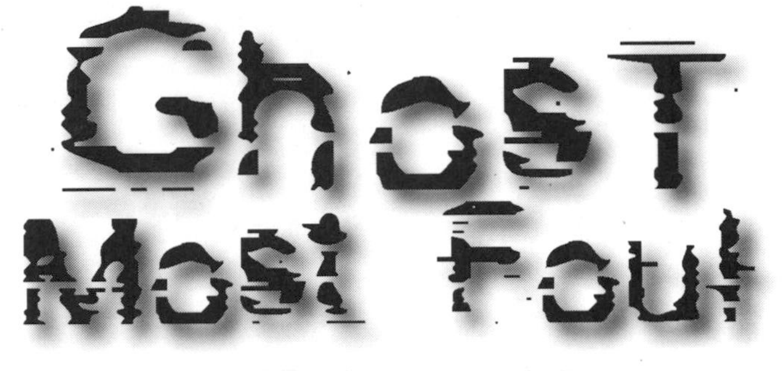

PATTI GRAYSON

www.coteaubooks.com

Ghost Most Foul

PATTI GRAYSON

Edited by Kathryn Cole
Cover designed by Jamie Olson
Typeset by Susan Buck
Printed and bound in Canada

Library and Archives Canada Cataloguing in Publication

Grayson, Patti, 1957-, author

Ghost most foul / Patti Grayson.

Issued in print and electronic formats.

ISBN 978-1-55050-614-3 (pbk.).--ISBN 978-1-55050-615-0 (pdf).--
ISBN 978-1-55050-821-5 (epub).--ISBN 978-1-55050-822-2 (mobi)

I. Title.

PS8613.R39G46 2015 jC813'.6 C2014-908232-0
C2014-908233-9

Library of Congress Control Number 2014955929

COTEAU BOOKS

2517 Victoria Avenue
Regina, Saskatchewan
Canada S4P 0T2
www.coteaubooks.com

Available in Canada from:
Publishers Group Canada
2440 Viking Way
Richmond, British Columbia
Canada V6V 1N2

Available in the US from:
Orca Book Publishers
www.orcabook.com
1-800-210-5277

10 9 8 7 6 5 4 3 2 1

Coteau Books gratefully acknowledges the financial support of its publishing program by: the Saskatchewan Arts Board, The Canada Council for the Arts, the Government of Canada through the Canada Book Fund, the City of Regina, and the Government of Saskatchewan through Creative Saskatchewan.

Canada Council for the Arts Conseil des Arts du Canada

For Phil & Miranda

PROLOGUE

In some bizarre way that I don't understand, I was connected from the moment of impact. My brain must have sensed the shockwave even though I was sound asleep at the time. The explosion in the engine and the force of that much metal crashing into the dark ocean must have been horrific. Somehow, that disturbance ripped across thousands of kilometres to reach me. My dad says shortwave radio signals criss-cross the globe. No one hears them travelling through the air; nevertheless, they arrive in his basement workshop. So why couldn't that no-longer-audible explosion sound have awakened me? Maybe I was tuned in to her frequency. Other than the accident, what could have shot me bolt upright in bed and caused my heart to beat faster than it ever had before, on the basketball court or anywhere? What – other than some inexplicable connection to the crash – could have caused the sensation that part of me was being wrenched away to find her, leaving emptiness behind?

I know how Mom would explain it... "Oh, Summer, you're being silly. It was Christmas Eve," she'd say. "You ate too many chocolates from the Pot of Gold box before you went to sleep. Overexcited and dreaming. Remember the Christmas Eve when you were five and you swore you woke up to Santa's bells right over your bedroom ceiling?" And then she'd laugh, not her silent, hold-your-aching-ribs laugh when she thinks something is absolutely hilarious, but her nervous laugh that's more like a giggling hiccup – the laugh that borders on an apology.

My mother has as many laughs as the Inuit have words for snow. That's partly why I haven't told her about what I've been seeing. It's not a laughing matter. The other reason is that she's a triage nurse at Garvin Hospital Emergency, and if she discovered I took a basketball to the head shortly before the apparition appeared the first time, she would freak out.

I can see it right now. It's hovering around the scoreboard, wispy and undefined one moment and then pulsing with iridescent brightness the next. Since we started this game, the scoreboard has gone blank a half-dozen times. The scorekeepers check the electrical plugs and start pushing buttons. When the power comes back, they have to reset the score, causing time outs because the refs have to confirm everything is correct before we can start playing again. I am light-headed from the scent of coconut wafting over me every few minutes. And I feel guilty of an undefined offence, as if the score sheet should show that I have enough personal fouls to be thrown out of the game. Fouled out because of a ghost. I turn my back to the bleachers so my parents can't see me gulping for air. I need to focus on the ball in my hands and the hoop in front of me...just the ball and the hoop...and nothing else.

CHAPTER ONE

Sweat trickled from my hairline down the side of my face. I used my t-shirt sleeve to wipe it off and saw Karmyn and Roxx doing the same. I glanced up at the gymnasium clock – ten minutes remaining in the practice. It was my best yet! My left-handed layups were finally going into the hoop, and I'd shot eight out of ten from the foul line. For the first time since the start of the school season, Karmyn and Roxx had asked me to be in their group for a passing drill. They usually paired up and never invited a third in unless Coach made them. I squeezed hard on my water bottle and gulped the last dregs of liquid. Coach Nola Blythe blew her whistle. The whole team hustled to the jump-ball circle in the middle of the gym, all except CJ and Faith, who started dribbling their basketballs and talking about the movie they were going to after practice.

Coach Nola watched them saunter in and then said, "Ladies, how long have you known me?" She didn't wait for a response. "Some of you attended my first basketball clinic this past summer at Parks and Rec, right?"

A few of us nodded.

She continued, "And the rest of you…how long have I been your coach? Just over a month? That's long enough for you to know my expectations. Granted, it's the last practice before Christmas, and some of you are overexcited, but let's review this, shall we? When I blow the whistle, what does it mean?"

We all chorused, "Hold the balls. Listen up."

Dodie, as usual, was the loudest. What she lacked in

basketball skills, she made up for in enthusiasm. Karmyn and Roxx shifted away from her, but Dodie either didn't notice or didn't care.

"Very good, ladies!" Coach Nola said. She lifted her ball, spun it on her pointer finger, and took a long hard look at CJ and Faith. It was as if the whole globe was spinning there on her fingertip, waiting for whatever command she might give it.

Faith broke the silence. "Sorry, Coach," she said, looking down at the floor. She snuck a sideways glance at CJ and then cast her eyes back down to the hardwood.

"Sorry," CJ added, but proceeded to dig a lip gloss tube out of her shorts pocket and furtively reapply it while still holding her basketball in her other hand.

Coach Nola grinned. "Thank you, ladies, but you both know *sorry* doesn't cut it in *my* gym. Do it thrice! That's one, two, three times around," she said, tracing large circles in the air with her finger.

CJ dropped her lip gloss back into her pocket, and she and Faith proceeded to run the laps while the rest of us stretched. Coach Nola rotated on the spot, watching the girls circle the gym. Twice, in a burst of speed, legs pumping, shoes digging into the floor, Coach dribbled to the three-point line, jump-shot, swished and then ran back to where we sat.

She called out to CJ, who was starting to lag behind Faith, "Pick it up please, CJ. Double time. Last lap. The rest of these ladies want to go home."

Both girls came panting back into our midst and collapsed beside us.

"Good job. Good hustle," she told the two of them. "In the new year, my expectation is that *no one* will be running extra laps for me. It won't be necessary, hmmm? You have all come a long way, with your skills and self-discipline. I'm super proud of you." She smiled. It wasn't just a smile, it was a power smile. If you could have harnessed Coach Nola Blythe's smile energy at that moment, you could have switched off the school breakers and not experienced an interruption in the hydro supply.

"Okay, on your feet, everyone."

We all stood and formed a semi-circle in front of her. She thrust her hand forward, fist clenched, and demanded, "Who are we?"

"Garvin Invaders!" we shouted back.

"What's our game?"

"B-ball!"

She smiled again. "Okay, remember I told you at the beginning of the season that I always have a plan? When I took this team on, what was my plan?"

Karmyn's hand shot up.

"Yes, Karmyn?"

"Your plan was to get us moving on the court and improve our skills."

"Excellent," Coach said.

Karmyn pushed some stray strands of hair off her face and looked smug. Her mother was dating the man who had coached the Garvin Varsity boys' basketball team for years, and everyone thought Karmyn was our best player. She'd been captain of our Grade Seven team the year before. Sometimes, I felt that if she didn't have her cascading red hair, people wouldn't notice her as much, but it was hard to look anywhere else when Karmyn was around, and she knew it. As much as I envied her, I longed to be included in her and Roxx's circle.

Coach Nola turned to me. "And Summer," she began, "do you think as a team, we're succeeding in the plan?"

Any time Coach Nola talked directly to me, I felt as if my tongue was too big for my mouth. I wanted to say how our fast break was finally fast, and how we were learning to stay between our man and the basket on defence. I wanted to show her that I knew as much as Karmyn, but all I could do was nod and say "Yes!" My ponytail bobbed behind my head like a spring.

"Anyone disagree with Summer?" Coach Nola asked.

"No!" everyone chorused.

"Good," she said. "I agree with Summer, too. This brings me to a wonderful place as your coach...the chance to enhance our plan before the game season is even underway."

We all looked at each other expectantly, except for Trish, who often looked to her twin as if she might need Tracy to translate for her, even though Tracy seldom seemed to notice. As usual, no one really looked at Dodie. Dodie, who was adjusting the elastic strap that holds her glasses in place during practice, beamed and was open to the slightest eye contact from anyone.

"Here's the plan enhancement," Coach began. "I think this team can be good enough by the end of season to win the Grade Eight Provincial Championship."

Our mouths fell open. There was utter disbelief. A flutter swelled in my stomach.

Coach Nola raised her hand to regain our attention. "Ladies, I'm going to quote Michael Jordan, arguably the best basketball player of all time. He said, 'You have to expect things of yourself before you can do them.' So *your* time has come to start having expectations!" She looked at each one of us in turn, then declared, "This team is going to be a concrete monolith when the competition comes at us. And we, the Garvin Invaders, are going to invade their territory – especially those big Winnipeg city teams!"

We all started babbling at once. Karmyn and Roxx reminded each other that the Grade Seven provincial champs – the Westun Wolverines – had a player who had scored thirty points against us in a single game the previous year. CJ grabbed Faith's arm and asked her if the Grade Eight boys played their provincial finals in the *same* gym complex on the *same* weekend. While Dodie stood, bouncing on her toes, saying "Wow," Val asked her if she thought they'd serve taco-in-a-bag at the Provincial Final canteen. Tracy flipped her long braid over her shoulder and said there had been twins on the championship team a few years earlier. Trish asked if they were identical. And I ventured to ask Coach how we could possibly win Provincials when we'd had a winless record the previous year.

Coach Nola shouted over our voices, "It's going to take some work, ladies. Are you willing to W-O-R-K?"

"Y-E-S!" we howled.

"Okay, when I ask you, 'What's our plan?' you will answer, 'Invade and win!' Got that?"

We nodded.

"Who are we?" she shouted.

"Garvin Invaders!"

"What's our game?"

"B-ball!"

"What's our plan?"

"Invade and Win!"

Coach Nola had a big grin on her face, and her dark eyes flashed with such mirth that we couldn't help but high-five each other as if we were already the provincial champs.

She raised her hand again to quieten us. "One last thing before you all go and eat too much turkey over the break. Oh, maybe two last things… First, I'll be dining on tropical fruits on my Caribbean holiday, so you ladies eat some healthy food, too, okay? Athletes require good nutrition!"

CJ and Faith exchanged looks behind Val's back. Val battled her weight and was the slowest of us all on the court. She was still a better player than Dodie.

Coach continued, "And secondly, one of the reasons – *not* the exclusive or most important reason, because each one of you brings something special to this team – but *one* of the reasons I think this team can win the provincials is our Secret Weapon, that's our S.W., Summer Widden."

Everyone turned to look at me. Roxx whooped, "Yay, Summer!"

I felt a rush of gratitude toward both Coach Nola and Roxx.

Coach explained, "I think Summer has the best

rebounding potential of anyone her age I've seen. She already uses her height to full advantage and instinctively boxes out, denying the opposition access to the boards. Generally, Grade Eight girls don't make a high percentage of their shots, so rebounding is key. For that reason – and a few others I'll go over with you in the New Year – I'm naming Summer our captain for this season. Look for her leadership come January!"

There were audible gasps.

Coach Nola ignored them. "Balls away in the equipment room. Have a happy holiday, and when you step onto the hallowed court in the new year, step on as *winners*, and when you step off the hallowed court, step off as *winners*! You girls should know that I'm proud to be the coach of each and every one of you!" She turned on her heel and headed for the gym office.

No one moved for what seemed like an eternity. Everyone glanced from Karmyn to me and back again. I could feel my face turning the colour of Karmyn's hair. I stared down at my ball until I could see a universe in each tiny pebbled dimple. Karmyn made the first move. I held my breath as she slammed her ball down on the gym floor, stomped to the girls' change room and kicked the door open. Roxx, who moments before had cheered for me, retrieved Karmyn's ball, took it to the equipment room along with her own, then jogged straight for the change room after Karmyn. I sensed that Dodie and Val were smiling at me, but I didn't dare look. CJ, Faith and the twins put their balls away and followed Roxx. Mine was the last ball in. I stood in the equipment room pretending that the balls needed rearranging on the rack. Eventually, I heard the last of the girls leave the change room. The clang of the metal latch echoed through the empty gymnasium behind them. I hurried into the change room, shoved my street clothes on top of my sweaty gym wear and sprinted toward the opposite exit.

As I rushed past the gym office, Coach Nola stepped out.

"Summer!" she said. I had to stop and face her. She looked hard at me. Sometimes when she looked at me like that, it was as if she were running a scanner over the bar code of my deepest thoughts, because the next thing she'd say would be exactly what I needed to hear.

"You deserve to be captain. You know that, don't you? You're going to be the positive leader these girls need."

"Thanks." I managed to breathe the word out.

"Oh, and Summer," she said, and then paused to zip on her warm-up jacket. "We've enhanced the plan, right?"

I nodded.

Her eyes flashed determination. "So, you know that old expression 'It's not whether you win or lose, it's how you play the game'? Well, the first thing *my* captain has to learn is Nola Blythe's version. It's a smidgen different. I want you to repeat it to yourself over the entire holiday. Repeat it when you're eating turkey, when you're brushing your teeth, when everyone else is singing 'Auld Lang Syne.' Ready?" she asked.

I nodded.

"It's not *whether* you win or lose, it's *how* you *win* the game." Then she winked at me and grinned. A power grin. "From watching you thus far, I have a feeling that deep inside you dwells that knowledge already. It's a mature knowledge, and one that, once again, points to you as the best choice for captain of this team. I'll see you in the New Year." She turned and closed the gym office door behind her.

CHAPTER TWO

Two days later was Christmas Eve, and although I felt as if I'd already received the best gift ever from Coach Nola, I was growing excited. Not as excited as my older sister, Holly, who still acted like a kid when it came to Christmas, birthdays and any other holidays. You'd think I was the one attending first-year college and she was in Grade Eight. Holly loved secrets. When she had one, it was as if it started vibrating inside her until she looked like one of those cans being shaken on the paint-mixing machine at the hardware store – her spiky, pixie hair all a-tremble on top of her head. She couldn't contain a secret for long before hints started spilling out of her.

The two of us were hanging glass angels on our Christmas tree. The fresh balsam smell was like a balm for the dry furnace-fed air. Outside, snow was falling in huge wet flakes, melting down the glass pane of the living room window.

Holly glanced over her shoulder to make sure Mom and Dad were out of earshot and then whispered, "Oh Summer, you're going to l-o-v-e all your Christmas presents. It's almost like a theme, you know? And it's so cool because they are so perfect for you; I mean, not everyone would want them. You won't believe it, but Mom actually shopped online at some tall girls' shop in the States. And Dad bought you something on eBay! They paid exchange and shipping. But mine's the best. Wait till you open it!"

Just then, Mom started down the stairs, carrying an armful of presents to put under the tree. She had them stacked up to her chin and was stretching to peer over the packages so she wouldn't miss the next step as she descended. Holly and I jumped up to help her.

"Oh, thank you girls," Mom said. "Don't ever do what I just did. I could have broken my neck."

I peeked at name tags on the packages as we placed them under the tree. From Holly's hints, I had a fairly good idea what might be in mine.

"Girls, you've made the tree look just beautiful. The best yet!" Mom exclaimed.

Dad came up from the basement workshop carrying his old cassette player and proceeded to try to rewind it to the exact start of Bing Crosby and David Bowie singing "Little Drummer Boy." Each time he stopped and hit the play button, snippets of *ra-pum-pum-pums* and *I played my drums* blasted out. I took the opportunity to shake, rattle and sniff all my packages. Mom watched and then laughed as if I was entirely too silly. As she headed back upstairs for more packages, Dad retold the story of how he could never find that particular recording of "Little Drummer Boy" in stores, so one year he recorded it from the television by holding a microphone to the TV speaker.

"Sounds like it, too!" Holly said, snickering. "Dad, no one would believe that you're the electrical shop teacher! We have a cassette player instead of a surround-sound system. And our Christmas lights blink on and off and then stay off for no apparent reason."

Dad replied, "Our old things work just fine. We're being environmentally responsible and not buying into the crass commercial economy." He took his glasses off and polished them with his shirttail. One corner of his frames was held together by a tiny piece of red electrical wire instead of the original screw. He squinted at the Christmas tree and added in a mock stern tone, "By the looks of things, you girls have way too many presents this year."

After Dad played "Little Drummer Boy" three or four times, he and Mom headed into the kitchen for eggnog and a shrimp ring. I wanted to question Holly outright if Dad had managed to find a women's size basketball for me and whether Mom had actually bought me a Los Angeles Sparks #9 jersey. That was Lisa Leslie's number, my favourite player in the WNBA, and I wanted it so badly. I would have known by how rapidly Holly was pulsating whether or not the gift from the tall girl shop was my coveted jersey.

Holly picked a package with her name on the tag, shook it gently and then dropped it back under the tree like it was a hot potato. She smiled at me and I knew that she loved the anticipation and the uncertainty of what might be under the wrapping paper. I decided I didn't want to ruin my Christmas morning by knowing ahead of time, either. But instead of loving the anticipation, I found it was driving me crazy.

I tried to distract myself by repeating Coach's quote. "It's not *whether* you win or lose, it's *how* you *win* the game." It was a strange expression. If you thought about it really hard, it didn't quite make sense, but one thing was certain. There was no room for *losing* in it. You couldn't allow yourself to think about losing if you wanted to be a provincial champ. Imagining us winning the championship title rivalled Christmas anytime! But there was still the little problem of Karmyn's reaction to my being named captain. What if the girls were all really mad at me? They had never paid much attention to me before. I just rounded out the team. I wasn't an all-star like Karmyn, but unlike Dodie, I didn't drop the ball when it was passed to me, either. For two days, I'd been telling myself that Coach would help me handle it in the new year. I doubted that anyone on our team could be mad with her decision for long; she would convince them she was right. She had this persuasive, powerful air about her. None of us had ever met anyone like her before. One night, when Holly picked me up from practice and saw Coach Nola Blythe for the first time, she said, "Oh my gosh!

She's like a cross between an Amazon and a goddess! If I played on her team, I wouldn't know whether to run for my life or bow down at her feet!" It was still unbelievable that someone like her would move to Garvin and coach our little team. Thinking of Coach Nola reminded me of something.

"Dad," I called to him in the kitchen, "do you think you can fix our VCR over the holiday? Our coach told us that it would be really good to record some basketball games and watch them over and over – kind of like the way you listen to Bing and Bowie. We're supposed to pick out plays and watch different players' techniques."

Dad returned to the living room munching on a shrimp. "Well, if Ms. Blythe said so, then I'd better snap to it. I don't want to run gym laps come January because of my delinquent VCR repair service." He saluted me, military style. "How many laps for being late for practice?" he asked, trying to remember what I'd told him at the start of season.

"Ten!" I replied.

"And how many for talking while Coach is talking?"

"Fifteen!"

"Remind me, what is the biggest number of laps for?" he asked.

"If she hears you say anything like *we're losers*. Anything negative…it's twenty-five laps on your lunch break."

"Ouch!" Dad winced and limped toward Mom, who was carrying a tray with a big box of Pot of Gold chocolates and crystal punch cups filled with eggnog. He added, "Unrepaired VCRs must be punishable with a hundred laps or more!"

Mom set the tray down on the coffee table. She said, "Your Coach Nola will have forgotten all about laps after ten days in the Caribbean sun! She'll come back tanned and on island time!"

"You don't know her," I said. "She promised when break was over, we'd be working harder than ever."

Dad's limp became more exaggerated. He panted his way

over to the cassette player to restart "Little Drummer Boy." "Two hundred laps to the team captain for not watching basketball tapes on her broken VCR!" he shouted.

"Paul, stop teasing Summer!" Mom said. She tried hard not to, but she couldn't hold back her I-know-I-shouldn't-be-laughing laugh. Dad looked more like Quasimodo than someone who had just run laps. Holly threw a sofa cushion at him and echoed Mom's laughter.

As usual, I was the last to join in. *Summer, the serious one.*

CHAPTER THREE

A gymnasium. My teammates. There is only one light fixture. Instead of a light bulb, it has a miniature sun in it. The sun switches off. Absolute darkness. Someone expects us to continue shooting at the basket. I know I'll never sink a shot without that sun's illumination. Panic.

It was as if I was hurled out of the dream. I jolted upright in bed. My pulse sped. A war dance thumped in my chest. *Ka-thunk, ka-thunk, ka-thunk.* I wondered if my pounding heart could crack a rib. There was a strange hollowness in my ears, as if I'd just heard a harrowing noise, and a sickly taste on my tongue, like seaweed or salty brine. I tried to take long deep breaths, but the more I attempted to relax, the worse I felt. I scrambled out of bed and rushed to my window. The glow from the street light offered some comfort.

Outside, the weather had changed. There were no longer fluffy snowflakes drifting down. A howling north wind rioted – flurrying smaller hard flakes. The north sides of the tree trunks were plastered with snow. I could barely make out the houses across the street. Only the odd strand of Christmas lights twinkled bravely, while the ones strung on the tall cedar below my window quivered against the wind's assault. I pressed the side of my face to the chilly windowpane and rolled my forehead against it. I wanted to run to my parents' room and wake them, but I knew Mom had to work Christmas night. She needed her sleep.

What was wrong with me? This feeling was worse than any nightmare I'd ever had. Was it just the wind that had wakened me? That would be the simple natural explanation. But I didn't feel natural. It was as if the north wind had whipped some part of me right out of my body and was carrying it away.

I can go to Holly's room, I thought. *She wouldn't even wake if I crawled under her duvet.* Holly turned into a rock after midnight. Middle-of-the-night thunderstorms and emergency phone calls for Mom never woke her. "She sleeps the sleep of the clear conscience," Dad was known to say. Sometimes I wondered where that left me. I often woke at night worrying about an unfinished school assignment, or about some boy in the hallway who had asked me – to the amusement of his friends – "How's the weather up there?" It was easier at school before my crazy growth spurt. Everyone pretty much ignored me before that, which, for the most part, suited me fine.

I stood at the window and forced myself to remember it was Christmas Eve. The glowing red numbers on my alarm clock read 3:46 a.m. I would be able to open my presents in a few more hours. The tingle of anticipation didn't spread through my stomach like I expected it would. Instead, I felt emptiness. The north wind seeped in around my window frame. I couldn't tell if it was the cold air or fear that was chilling my bones. I shuddered and longed for the warmth of my dream's miniature sun. I lunged for my desk lamp and switched it on.

Light spilled over the one framed photo I kept on my desk – last year's school basketball team. I clutched the frame with both hands as if it could steady me. There we were, first-time team players, in our oversized forest green T-shirts. We were lined up in two rows. Karmyn, Roxx, CJ, Faith and I stood behind the twins, Trish and Tracy, who were kneeling front and centre with Dodie and Val on either side. Karmyn was the only one on the team at the start of that year who knew all the rules. Even in the photo, she was the easiest to pick out, with her flaming red curls. She looked ignitable, as if she could scorch everyone else in the photo.

The picture was taken after our best game in our only tournament. We had managed to hold the point spread down to twenty. It was also the final game of our season, since we hadn't made any playoffs in our own school division. Mrs. Svencheski, the school secretary who was also our coach, had thrown her little rule book into the air and said we deserved medals for that game because "we played our hearts out." On our way home to Garvin, she bought us all slushies at a Winnipeg convenience store and made us forget, for a while, that we were the worst bunch of basketball losers in our school division and beyond.

What changes had happened since that picture was taken! In the photo, I was the tallest by only a tiny margin. Less than a year later, I was almost a head taller than Karmyn and Roxx. And Karmyn Tait was no longer the captain. I was. Never before had I been named captain or leader of anything! Best of all was imagining our photo at the end of our Grade Eight season. We'd be sporting 2008 Provincial Championship medals, standing next to Coach Nola.

A huge gust of wind rattled my window. I was freezing from the inside out, and my teeth started to chatter. The desk lamp flickered. The hydro lines were likely covered in ice. I yanked the quilt off my bed and wrapped it around me, tucking the bottom under my feet and tightening the top around my chin. Down in the living room, the mantel clock chimed a mournful four a.m. The clock had such a sad, solemn sound, as if marking the passage of that hour was an unbearable burden.

The empty feeling seemed to be growing stronger. I needed to fill it up; maybe it was just a hunger craving. I thought of the Pot of Gold chocolates – my Christmas favourite ever since I could remember. Mom and Dad tempted me with almond bark, truffles, fudge, but all I wanted at

Christmas were the *rainbow chocolates*. I liked their too-sweet fillings and what I called the little suit-of-clubs nut cluster.

I opened my bedroom door. The scent of balsam stirred my nostrils and seemed to calm me. Deep breaths. I started down the stairs in the dark. I could make out the silhouette of the Christmas tree in front of the window; the swirling whiteness from outside added illumination to the living room. Silver and gold foil wrapping paper glistened at the foot of the tree. Chocolates…straight ahead on the coffee table. The brown wrapper cups rustled as I dug through to find a full one. I put several candies into my mouth at once. The wind still howled outside, but the chocolate was blissful. I sidled over to the tree and stroked its balsam needles. I inhaled the cleansing scent of evergreen, swallowed the mouthful of sweets and began to feel better.

Right beside me was one of my larger presents. I picked it up and shook it. It didn't make any noise at all, but I could feel a shifting in the box. I wondered if it was a basketball. It was about the right weight. If I could just see the outside of the box, maybe it would confirm that for me. Slipping my finger under the flap of taped paper, I gently pried it. The tape eased off. I unfolded the wrapped end and peeked inside. It was impossible to see anything in the dim glow from the outside light, so I reached over and plugged in the Christmas tree. Holding the opened end near the coloured lights, I peered at the indistinguishable writing on the box.

"Summer! What are you doing?"

The hall light switched on and I squinted against its brightness. My mother stood at the bottom of the stairs, hands on her hips. To avoid the look of astonishment on her face, I focused on the pattern of penguins performing figure eights all over the length of her flannel nightie.

"Summer, answer me. What are you doing?"

"I had a nightmare, Mom!" Pathos was what I was attempting.

"I can't believe what I'm seeing! Never would I have suspected that, that..." she stammered.

"But I did have a nightmare... It was more than a nightmare," I insisted, sticking the flap back down and sliding the parcel out of my reach. When she didn't answer, I said, "I didn't see a thing, Mom. I wasn't trying to open it, honest."

"To bed, young lady. I'm disappointed to find you sneaking around like this..."

I ran back upstairs and jumped into bed, hoping to hear a muffled giggle as Mom turned out the lights behind me. All I heard were her slippered foosteps padding down the hallway – and the north wind moaning more desperately than before.

CHAPTER FOUR

a water bottle
a sports bag
a t-shirt with *Swish* written across the shoulder
wrist sweatbands
three pairs of white ankle socks
a basketball-shaped pencil sharpener
a mini hoop and ball for the back of my bedroom door
a real leather women's Spalding basketball
a Los Angeles Sparks jersey, #9
a Steve Nash autographed Team Canada Olympic poster, framed

Those were my Christmas presents from Mom and Dad!

And from Holly: season tickets to Herdsmen basketball, including tickets to the Agassiz Invitational, their annual university tournament played over Christmas break.

I sat in the middle of my opened packages and couldn't believe my eyes. As if my family hadn't purchased it all for me, I kept lifting one item, putting it down, lifting another, and saying "Look at this! Isn't this awesome?"

After much smiling and laughing, Mom sighed. "I just hope this basketball thing isn't another fleeting fad – like Pokémon sticker books."

Dad said, "Oh, I don't think you have to worry, Olivia. Unless, of course, Summer decides to take up break-and-enter as her next hobby. I've heard she's quite skilled at sneaking around in the dark!"

"Mom! You didn't tell Dad. I didn't even see anything! I didn't feel well after my nightmare, and…"

Holly chimed in. "Yes, I think I'll cure my nightmare by opening a present at four a.m.!"

"You told Holly, too?"

Mom's answer was a nasal whinny.

"Holly, you should talk!" I protested. "You practically told me what was in every one of my presents – whether I wanted to know or not."

"I did not," Holly said and started folding her new sweaters. "I didn't tell you one single thing."

"Holly reveal a secret?" said Dad. "Never!"

I cried out, "Never? She always tells!"

"I do not!" she insisted and looked the picture of angelic innocence.

"That's enough girls," Mom clapped her hands at us as if she was shooing chickens. "Summer, I've never known Holly to ruin a surprise."

Holly primped her short spiky hair and smiled so hard that her gums showed.

How could they give me all those super presents and then make me so angry in one single morning? Christmas morning. A liquid edge of the empty feeling from the previous night started to seep over my skin. What was it? It had faded a bit in the excitement of opening presents, but it had never left me completely. I wished I could shake like a wet dog and be rid of it.

Then the phone rang.

"Merry Christmas!" Mom answered. "Oh, hello, Martha! Where are you calling from?... Oh, that's too bad… Listen, why don't you join us for Christmas dinner then? You won't have a thing prepared… We have plenty. It's just the four of us this year… Great! Come around three o'clock."

Holly said, "Who was that, Mom?"

"That was Martha, our X-ray tech. She was calling to let me know that their ski holiday had to be postponed, so she can take emergency calls if need be. The RCMP closed the #1 highway last evening with the blizzard."

"Mom," I said, feeling worse by the moment. "You mean Martha Direland, Dodie's mother?"

"That's right."

"And you invited them here today? Mrs. Direland is going to start in on how Dodie and I should be best friends, the way she did the day we saw them in the mall."

"Summer, it's Christmas Day." Mom's voice was tinged with a slight warning.

Ignoring the edge in her tone, I pressed on. "I do not want to spend Christmas dinner with Dodie Direland!"

Holly scrunched her nose at me. "What's wrong with Dodie?"

Dad patted the sofa so that I'd sit beside him. "Isn't Dodie on your basketball squad this year?" he asked.

"Yes, she's on our *team*, Dad. But she can't play. I think Coach only kept her to ensure we had enough subs if someone was sick or injured. There are only nine of us with Dodie. Coach has to spend extra time correcting everything she does. And she has this unnerving enthusiasm, like she has no awareness of how bad she is."

"Maybe Ms. Blythe sees potential in her if she has a positive attitude," Dad remarked.

"The private school Dodie attended before they moved here focused on hockey, so she still barely knows how to dribble, and she hasn't made a single free throw from the foul line yet!"

Mom cut in. "That's not very generous of you, Summer. Her mother is a great asset to our staff. She mentioned at work that Dodie has had a hard time fitting in over the past year. It wouldn't hurt you to be welcoming and support her on the team. Maybe you could become good friends."

"Tell that to the other girls, Mom. They're the ones who are always snickering behind Dodie's back."

"Poor kid," Holly chimed in.

Ignoring Holly's sympathetic murmurs, I continued, "One day I overheard Karmyn saying to Roxx, 'Doesn't Dodie just suck on the court? She's so bad we'll be lucky if she doesn't score on our *own* basket this year.'" I grabbed a toss cushion off the sofa and buried my chin and mouth in it to stop myself from saying anything more – to keep from admitting to my family I was afraid of becoming the next team target.

"Oh!" Mom said in a sarcastic drawl. "Well, if the *other* girls say mean things about Dodie, they must be true, and she must truly deserve them."

I bent the cushion around my ears and hoped that Mom wouldn't start in with "If the other girls jumped off a cliff, would you follow?"

Instead, she said, "Well, Dodie is your guest today, and I expect you to make an effort to be nice, and if that means going to your room to think about it, then maybe you should. And maybe have a little nap while you're at it. I don't think you slept enough last night."

I couldn't believe I was being semi-grounded on Christmas Day. Things were not turning out the way they should, and I was afraid to go back to my room, where the strange empty feeling might take full hold again. I also wanted to point out to Mom that Dodie was not *my* guest; Mom was the one who invited her. My throat tightened. No way was I going to cry. Pulling my Sparks jersey over my pyjamas, I bundled my mini hoop and ball, and dashed up the stairs two at a time. I hung the hoop on my door, backed up to the bed and started shooting: *Ka-thunk. Ka-thunk. Ka-thunk. KA-THUNK. KA-THUNK.* If I was going to be sent to my room, I might as well continue shooting all day and right through dinner. Dodie Direland and her family could just go fly a kite in a blizzard for all I cared. If the rest of the team found out I spent Christmas

Day with Dodie, they would think we were friends, which could be disastrous for me. I'd had enough of senseless jeers back in elementary school, *Summer, Summer. Shows her bummer!* Kids sniffed me out as an easy target for some reason, maybe because I had a tendency to cry too often in kindergarten. I'd discovered, since then, that if you did little and said less, you were likely to avoid negative attention. I had found it easy to be "beige" on the outside even when my inside colours were rioting. If Karmyn and Roxx got the idea that I was close to Dodie, I might as well break out in a rash of lime green and purple spots.

When the doorbell rang, I was determined to stay in my room. Mom's voice was filled with holiday cheer as she beckoned the Direlands inside. They let in a cold draught that I could feel all the way up the stairs and under the edge of my bedroom door. Dad knocked on it twice and entered.

"Summer, our guests are here," he said. I could tell by the way he looked at me over the top of his glasses that I shouldn't argue. He'd spent the afternoon shovelling out the driveway, which always put him in a bad mood. There was no choice but to go down and greet the Direlands.

I was wearing my oldest jeans and a t-shirt I normally reserved for painting the fence, but I couldn't resist slipping my new Sparks jersey overtop. Slouching, I headed down the stairs.

Dodie was sitting in the living room, looking at our tree. When she saw me, she said a quick hi, raising one hand out of her lap and flicking it upwards in a kind of lame wave. She was wearing a burgundy velvet dress with a matching bow in her hair, the same kind of outfit she wore when the science fairs were on at our school. She won the gold ribbon last year, so her photo was published in the school newsletter and local paper. I considered that a punishment, not a reward. A person could survive winning the geek prize, but to be dressed like that when you won it would be too humiliating!

"Hey, Dodie," I said, loud enough for my parents to hear above the commotion of mixing drinks and setting out fancy hors d'oeuvres.

Mrs. Direland turned from the kitchen doorway. "Oh, hello Summer!" she said. "Where's your sister?"

I answered, "Holly is probably still blow-drying her hair."

"You must be taller than your big sister now!" Mrs. Direland beckoned her daughter. "Dodie, come stand back to back with Summer."

Dodie, looking down at her hands, replied, "She's way taller, Mom."

"I know she's taller, Dodie. Let's see by how much." Mrs. Direland was a landmass of a woman herself.

"Mom…" Dodie started.

"Be a sport!" Mrs. Direland snipped.

Dodie stood behind me and didn't quite reach my shoulders.

"You have some distance to cover there, Dodie girl!" Mrs. Direland announced. "We'll definitely be increasing your protein and calcium intake."

Dodie sat back down and quietly said to me, "That's one *phat* jersey."

At first, I had to swallow a giggle that was welling up inside me. People dressed like Dodie should never say things like *That jersey is phat*. But immediately, I noticed that Dodie's normally high-volume enthusiasm was turned right down.

"Thanks, Dodie," I said. "I just got it this morning."

She nodded. Was it her dress or her mother that was making her so subdued?

"Dodie!" Mrs. Direland straightened her back. "How rude!"

I couldn't help but feel a little sorry for Dodie at that point. I said, "Dodie means it's really cool, Mrs. Direland. That's phat with a *ph*, not an *f*."

"That hardly improves it. We don't encourage slang in our

household. That jersey reminds me though…" Mrs. Direland's face turned even grimmer. "Olivia," she called. "Do you have a moment for some…some hospital business?"

My mom came out of the kitchen, looking puzzled. Mrs. Direland turned her head away from Dodie and me. "Don't mean to ruin the festivities Olivia, but if you have just a moment?" She swept Mom into the den and out of earshot.

I looked at Dodie. She gave a shrug, as if she was used to her mom having the latest gossip to share.

Holly came bounding down the stairs at that moment. "Hi Dodie, I'm Holly. You want to come to my room and listen to music or something?"

Dodie looked over at me. It was my turn to shrug.

Holly scowled a bit. "Come on, Summer. You're not going to stay down here until dinner's ready! Dad's going to put on 'Little Drummer Boy' any minute."

I nodded at Dodie and we all scampered up the stairs. As we headed into Holly's room, Dodie said, "I really do like your jersey. That's the team Lisa Leslie plays for, right?"

"Yeah," I said. "This is her number."

"Wow," Dodie said, breathing out her appreciation.

"Hey, wait," I said. "You have to see what my dad got me on eBay!" I rushed back down the stairs to retrieve my autographed Olympic poster from under the tree. The poster was tucked far behind, and as I crouched to reach it, Mom and Mrs. Direland came out of the den and headed into the kitchen.

I thought I overheard Mom say, "I don't know how I'll tell Summer…"

Tell Summer what? I wondered and then headed back upstairs to show Dodie my prized Christmas gift.

CHAPTER FIVE

The Direlands left late, and I was relieved to close my bedroom door behind them. The longer Dodie had stayed, the more enthusiastic she had become. At one point, I was wishing she'd revert back to the person sitting demurely by my Christmas tree with her hands in her lap. Allowing Dodie and my sister, Holly, to simultaneously occupy my bedroom – with no official limits on their chatter quotients – was enough to threaten the structural integrity of the walls! As soon as I was in my pyjamas, I scooped up my new basketball and decided to take it to bed with me. I'd heard of other athletes who slept with their basketballs as a kind of motivational technique: an eat, sleep, drink basketball strategy! I loved its pebbly surface and the new leather smell of it. I hoped that didn't mean I would soon be talking to it like Tom Hanks did with Wilson, the volleyball in the movie *Castaway*. Just as I set it beside my pillow, Mom knocked and opened my bedroom door.

"Good night," I called, expecting her to be rushing off to work the midnight shift at the hospital.

Instead, she came right in and sat at the foot of my bed. She reached over to switch on my desk lamp and took a deep breath.

I didn't wait for her to begin. "Holly and I were both nice to Dodie tonight, Mom. You don't have to lecture me about it."

Mom's mouth quivered into a slight smile and then dropped back down again. I sat up in bed. She hadn't come in to talk about Dodie, that was for certain. I reached for my basketball and clutched it to my chest. The basketball seemed to give Mom a focal point. She kept her eyes on it as she started.

"Summer, there's been some terrible news about your coach, Nola Blythe. Apparently, she was taking a private chartered aircraft from Puerto Rico to the island of St. Kitts, where she was to meet a friend. It's believed that the plane began to experience some navigational equipment problems. At the same time, an unexpected tropical storm developed. Her plane never made it."

"What do you mean – never made it?" I demanded. A wave of the dreadful emptiness I'd felt the night before sucked at me like a powerful undertow.

"The plane was lost, Summer."

"Lost?"

Mom slid her way forward from the foot of the bed. She set my basketball aside, so she could hold my hands in hers while she continued. "There was some wreckage debris discovered not far from St. Kitts. Apparently, the storm prevented full recovery efforts. I'm so sorry, Summer. I know how much you adored her."

A cement-like thirst hardened in my throat; I could barely squeeze out the words. "You mean, Coach Nola was killed?"

"It's fairly certain," Mom responded.

"But not definite then?"

"Well, Summer, there's been no body, of course." Mom's eyes darted to the basketball to avoid looking at me.

It was as if my whole bedroom was holding its breath, as if we would all suffocate if the room didn't start breathing again. I shook my head to try to force an inhalation. "Well…she could have survived then, Mom. She's so strong! She could have swum to safety. Don't planes have flotation seats and everything in case they have an emergency landing on water?"

"They believe the plane crashed, Summer. It wasn't an emergency landing."

"Who's *they?*" I demanded.

"I imagine the coast guard and airport officials in the

Caribbean. I believe both islands have international airports. I'm sure Ms. Blythe's family is doing everything they can to learn more. The poor souls..." Her voice trailed off.

"Did Mrs. Direland tell you this? Is that why she pulled you into the den?"

"Yes," Mom answered.

I swung my feet out of bed and clutched my basketball to my chest. "Mom, she's so bossy and mean toward Dodie. Maybe she's spreading wild gossip! Maybe none of this is true!"

"Your dad said they just confirmed it on a local news report," Mom said, her eyes following me as I paced the room.

"But how could they know so soon afterwards? It just happened last night, didn't it?" The words were out of my mouth before I realized what I was saying. I sat back down on my bed and pulled at my covers.

Mom looked at me quizzically. "How do you know that, Summer? Martha didn't say exactly when it happened. Which day? Or night? I don't know."

"I...well, it must have been because...because she had to arrive down there after our last practice, which was three days ago, and...I mean...when else could it have happened?" I was saying the words, but all I could think of was the way I'd woken so suddenly the night before, how I felt as if part of me was gone searching, the feeling in my ears, the taste in my mouth. Somehow there must have been a connection. Somehow. But I had no idea how.

Mom frowned. "Well, I suppose it doesn't really matter when it happened...the sad tragedy is that it did." Her voice sounded as if she might not continue, then she seemed to muster the strength to finish. She reached to stroke my hair the way she did when I was a little girl. One moment I longed for her to continue stroking until the buzzing in my head was tamed; the next moment, I swatted her hand away.

I blurted, "Why didn't you tell me the minute you knew?"

"Summer, we obviously wanted it confirmed to some

extent before we told you. You just said yourself that Martha might have been wrong." Mom had placed her hands in her lap and straightened her back.

"I could have confirmed it with someone myself," I ranted, knowing I wasn't making any sense, but suddenly feeling so angry at my mother I wanted to throw the basketball through my window. "She can't be dead. She can't be!" I shouted. "What about our team? What about her promise? 'I'll see you in the New Year!' Those were the very last words she said to me."

I wrenched myself farther away from my mother and drove my face into my pillow. My eyes and throat stung with the searing heat of the tears I was forcing myself not to cry.

I shouldn't cry for her. That would mean she was really dead. But what if I cried, and then we received the news that she was rescued? How exquisitely light my heart could feel then. Every tear would be worth it. Maybe if I could cry enough tears, they could fuel her rescue mission. My mind was racing with crazy thoughts! Tom Hanks was rescued in *Castaway*. It had to be possible. I *would* talk to Spalding, my basketball. I'd beg Spalding, beseech Spalding and pray to Spalding. We could somehow save Coach Nola's life, and she'd come back to us knowing that we'd saved her.

My tears spilled onto my pillowcase just as my dad poked his head through the bedroom doorway. When I didn't look up, he cleared his throat. Even though I couldn't see him, I imagined him removing his glasses, holding them to the light and wiping them on his shirttail. His voice held an unnatural hefty sound to it and broke off in the middle.

"Is there anything I can do here, Olivia? You're going to have to leave for work. Summer, can I sit…sit with you here for a bit?"

"No, Dad, I just want to be alone." The pillow muffled my words, so Mom had to repeat them.

"You're sure?" Dad asked.

I had to be alone. I had to focus all my energy on saving

Coach Nola. But even as I conjured rescue thoughts, I knew it was hopeless. I knew she was gone. It was Coach Nola's light that had been extinguished in my dream. The miniature sun. That's why I was playing in the dark; that's why I knew I couldn't make a shot in that darkness. Without her, we were nothing. We were just the basketball losers from last year.

Mom stood and spoke to Dad. "Summer said Ms. Blythe was so physically strong. Do you think, Paul, there is any chance she could survive?"

Dad sighed. "I hate to say it, but it is very unlikely."

Mom murmured in agreement. "Her poor family. Can you imagine what they must be going through?"

A pang of guilt stabbed deep. Even though I'd never met Coach Nola's family, I knew they must be in mourning. I was being so selfish thinking only of our basketball team. The hole inside me grew bigger.

Mom kissed the back of my head and shut the door behind her. I thought back to the day I met Coach Nola, how she had taught us dribble tag. I was able to knock everyone else's ball away while still maintaining control of my own to win the game.

"Well done!" she had said. "It's Summer, right? Where'd you learn such great ball control?"

As always, when she spoke to me, but especially that very first time, I couldn't seem to get my tongue to wrap itself around any words. I wanted to tell her that I'd been practising dribbling and shooting in my driveway every non-rainy day for the entire summer. But all I could manage was a blush, a shrug and "I...don't know, really."

That was the first time she had beamed at me. It was like a thunderbolt to the heart, it was so unexpected. She took a couple of steps toward me and said only loud enough for me to hear, "Well, Summer," she paused, considering her words, "That must be one of the reasons I'm supposed to be here – so that you will come to know."

At that moment, with her dark intense eyes on me, I secretly wondered if all my practising had somehow conjured Coach Nola.

I could hear my dad patter down the hall, stop and listen at my door and shuffle away again. The right thing to do would be to call him in. I knew he was worrying about me, but all I could do was wish for sleep, a sleep from which I could awaken and it would be that first day again. I rolled over in my bed and clutched my basketball. In between bouts of tears, I continued to beseech Spalding to generate a miracle.

CHAPTER SIX

"I'm already warming the car," Holly said, standing in the doorway to my bedroom in her new pink winter parka. "Why aren't you ready?"

"Holly, I told you, I don't want to go."

It was two days before New Year's, and I had barely left my room since the news of Coach's plane crash. I had refused to take phone calls as well, but that just made me realize what a loser I was, since there was only one phone call for me anyway. I hadn't checked my email. I didn't want to talk to anyone about Coach Nola.

Holly put on her authoritative voice, the one she probably used at college when her teachers asked her a question. "Summer, do you know how much I paid for the Herdsmen tickets? Quite a bit. And even though I don't have the slightest interest in basketball, I am willing to take you to the games. I could have just bought you a toque or something, you know?"

"Holly, why can't you understand right now?" I pleaded. I didn't want to see anyone playing basketball.

"And why don't you understand there are no refunds? And I have a lot of expenses at college. And I won't get a pay cheque until spring when I start working again."

"Okay, okay, give me five minutes and I'll be ready," I said.

Holly smiled and bobbed back down the stairs to wait for me. I ran a brush through my hair, put it in a ponytail, changed into a clean sweater and followed her down. I knew my plain appearance would irk Holly; she'd taken at least an hour to get ready to go, but after looking at me, she just smiled and out we went to Mom and Dad's chorus of "Drive carefully, Holly."

The roads had all been cleared since the Christmas Eve blizzard, but the world was still dressed in an overcoat of snow. The snowbanks were higher than the top of our car, and the evergreens were laden with a thick cotton-puff on every bough. Christmas lights twinkled right through the snow that buried them. The best part was when we reached the city of Winnipeg and we drove to the corner of Portage and Main. Christmas lights cascaded across the broad streets and seemed to escort us right to the university.

My spirits were lifting by the time we took our seats in the Buffalo Athletic Centre. Both sides of the stands were almost full, loud rap music pumped out of the speakers and the Herdsmen players were on the court at one end, warming up to take on the Assiniboine University Gremlins at the other end. Streaks and flashes of white and red warm-up jerseys at one hoop, green and yellow at the other. Over the loudspeaker, the announcer proclaimed that the Gremlins were in for a fright of their own tonight with the oncoming stampede of Buffalo Centre athletes. There was a loud cheer in response from the Herdsmen home side of the gymnasium. With that, one of the Gremlin players responded by slam-dunking and hanging on the rim for effect. A loud cheer rose from the visitor side of the gym.

I was so enveloped in the excitement that it took a few minutes to notice a guy seated next to Holly, holding her parka while she wiggled out of the sleeves. She was smiling at him adoringly. He was tall, had long, wavy blond hair below his ears and a clean-shaven chiselled face that seemed youthful yet classically ancient at the same time.

Holly caught me staring. "This is my…um…" She looked at the guy who smiled at her, and then she continued, "My new boyfriend, Everett. Ev, this is Summer, my basketball-crazed sister."

A hundred furies ran through me at once. So Everett was the reason Holly insisted we come to the game! Maybe he was the real reason I received season tickets. And how could she call me "basketball-crazed" when my coach had just died? Why was she so insensitive to what was happening in my life? My fury turned inward. Why did I let myself become so excited when we entered the centre? I could feel the basketball energy like it was something tangible and wearable and edible, and it made me forget and remember Coach Nola at the same time. I wanted to feel sad, but I could barely contain my exhilaration.

I forced myself to say a polite hello to Everett.

He reached over and shook my hand. "It's nice to meet you, Summer," he said. "Holly was so excited to get these tickets for you."

Holly interrupted. "So which one is your brother, Ev?"

"Number 22 on the Herdsmen. Baxter is first-year though, so he may not see much court time."

I blurted out, "Your brother is Number 22?"

"Yeah." Everett smiled again. He leaned forward past Holly to talk to me. "Tall, eh? He's six foot four. He was the top-ranked rebounder in the province in his two varsity years, and he had three offers to play university ball. He decided to stay home here in Winnipeg."

Holly announced, "You two talk basketball. I'm going to the ladies' room before the game starts."

Everett stood while she dashed out of her seat and up the bleachers. When he sat back down, I could feel myself blushing at being left alone with him.

He didn't seem to notice. "So, Holly said you had some really bad news over the holiday."

He said it in such a sympathetic way, I could feel the tears well up instantly, and before I could stop them they were splashing down my cheeks. I dashed them off my face, and Everett dug into his jacket pocket and produced a wad of fresh tissue.

How embarrassing to be bawling my eyes out in front of my sister's brand new boyfriend, whom I just met. It would serve Holly right if I chased him off! Where was Holly?

He said, "Hey, sorry about that. What a terrible thing to happen." He waited for me to blow my nose, and then said, "Baxter and I have had some great coaches, and I know how much I still miss some of them."

I snuffled into the tissue. "So you play, too?"

"Uh, not any more. I was never committed like Baxter. Practise, study, practise, go to classes, practise, study and try to find time to eat in there. No time for friends. No time for fun. Not my style."

"But basketball would be the fun! And your teammates are your friends," I said.

Everett laughed. "Holly was right. You've got the basketball bug, eh?"

I blushed again and giggled through my sniffles. Sitting there, anticipating the start of the game, I couldn't imagine how Everett could no longer be playing. It was all I wanted to do. I said, "You make it sound like you've been cured from the basketball disease!"

Everett looked at me with a mad scientist grin. "Yes, and I will become world famous when I develop the immunization. Then no one will ever have to suffer with the basketball sickness again." He added, "I will cure you, Summer!"

It was hard not to laugh at his contorted face. I said seriously, "So then, you're going to be a world-famous doctor – that's why you don't have time for basketball?"

It was Everett's turn to chuckle. "I don't imagine I'm going to be a world-famous anything, Summer. Right now, I'm taking a few philosophy and language courses and working part-time. I don't really know what I want to be when I grow up. Do you?"

I sighed. "I just want to play basketball."

Everett chuckled, nodding, and said, "That's what Baxter

answers when you ask him, too. But he's actually planning on a psychology degree so that he can become a sports psychologist."

I turned to watch Baxter on the court. His hair was cut really short with dyed tips. You could tell he was Everett's brother, except when it came to their intensity levels. Everett's demeanour was laid-back buttery leather, while Baxter's stance was taut, about-to-snap elastic.

"I think I can see him being a kind of frenzied advisor to world champions," I said.

Everett threw his head back and laughed. "I'll be sure to tell him that."

Carrying a big cardboard container of popcorn and three cold soft drinks, Holly plopped back down beside us in a wave of floral perfume – just in time for the game lineup. When the master of ceremonies announced Number 22, Baxter Lindell, we cheered as loud as we could, but not as loud as someone in the front seats.

Holly said to Everett, "I forgot your parents were here. Shouldn't we go sit with them?"

Everett shifted in his seat. "As a rule, I try not to. They become pretty intense." He said this in an apologetic tone, and then added, "It's easier if I sit somewhere else. They don't notice anyway."

Holly was lost for words for the first time since I could remember. Everett looked uncomfortable, slightly downcast. Holly passed him some popcorn and took a long sip of her soft drink.

I felt desperate to think of something to say. "That's okay, Everett," I started. "You should see how intense our dad gets about wires and plugs!"

Everett laughed, and Holly regained her perkiness. She slipped her arms through one of Everett's and said, "Parents, eh? Wild!"

The jump-ball whistle blew and the game was on! Baxter played for a few minutes in the first half and scored four points on offensive rebounds. In the second half there was less than a ten-point spread. The Herdsmen were losing, so Baxter sat on the bench while the senior players subbed in. Final score: Gremlins 74, Herdsmen 68. I knew it shouldn't matter so much, but I felt crushed inside. Everett seemed delighted though.

I dared to ask, "Did you want them to lose?"

He chuckled and said, "No way! I'm just happy because Baxter scored in the game and played some great defence. I think he managed three defensive rebounds along with his two baskets. He showed his stuff. He'll be pleased."

I wanted to ask Everett how he could be so sure. I was certain Baxter would be miserable with the night's loss, but I kept quiet. Holly was so happy that Everett was happy that she reached over and kissed him. I looked away while she told him that he should go see his brother and we would head home.

"You want to come and meet Baxter?" he asked.

I was about to squeal a definite yes, when Holly said, "No, it will have to be next time. With the slippery roads, Mom and Dad will worry if we're late."

Next time, I thought. But would there even be a next time? What would be the point of coming and torturing myself watching if my own team didn't even exist? It was the first time I realized that not only would Coach Nola be gone, but the entire future of our team was in jeopardy.

I looked around at the emptying bleachers. Popcorn and drink containers littered the stands. I looked out over the vacated court. The hardwood floors gleamed under the lights, but there was such an abandoned feeling to the space. I was suddenly overwhelmed by the now familiar aching emptiness inside me. All I could do was fill it with anger. *Why did you have to die?* The music blasting out of the loudspeakers as we made our way out of the Buffalo Centre was my only reply.

CHAPTER SEVEN

My return to school after the holidays was challenging. Mom had reminded me several times over the break that time heals, and she had been right. My initial excruciating misery had begun to fade as we passed into the new year. Returning to school and knowing I'd have to face my teammates brought it surging back. It was hard to explain why I'd made no effort to contact any of them. But I believed that if I told them what I wanted to tell them – how I woke in a panic the night Coach must have crashed, how I had some connection to her death – my teammates would think I was a freak, a liar or a self-centred creep.

On that first morning back, the school flag few at half-mast, and in the main hall, there wasn't the usual boisterous exuberance you would expect from students returning after holidays. Numerous small groups clustered together and talked in subdued voices until the bell rang for homeroom. After attendance, we were ushered straight to the gym for assembly. I stared at the floor, not wanting to look at the basketball hoops for fear I would start sobbing and make a fool of myself.

Principal Talbot talked about the tragic loss to our community. He said, "Although Ms. Blythe taught at the nearby elementary school, she took an active role within our junior high by coaching our girls' Grade Eight basketball team. I'm asking those particular girls to congregate in Mrs. Chamber's office after assembly." He concluded by requesting a moment of silence.

There were sniffles behind me. Clenching my teeth, I hardened myself against any overt show of sorrow.

Once I was out of the gym, I dragged my feet all the way to the counsellor's office – the last one to arrive. All the girls turned and looked at me, then turned back in the general direction of Mrs. Chamber, who was sitting cross-legged in her office chair, wearing one of her sweep-the-floor length denim skirts and a granola-coloured sweater. She began by saying that each one of us might grieve differently and that no one should judge someone else's response based on their own. That gave me the courage to sit down on the comfy couch next to the twins, who, along with Val, were the only ones crying. Karmyn sat, relaxed in a straight-back chair. Roxx sat beside her, sneaking looks out the window at the staff parking lot. She had dyed her hair over the holiday – an orange shade. It looked like a botched attempt to copy Karmyn's red hair. CJ was focused on a wall poster of a sunrise with the words *It's another beautiful day in paradise*. Faith sat picking at her nail polish. Dodie was the only one who looked as if she was really listening to our counsellor.

Mrs. Chamber then said, "Perhaps we'd like to all join hands and reflect for a moment on our collective loss."

When only the twins joined hands, Mrs. Chamber cleared her throat and added, "That's all right too. Instead, I invite you to ask questions or share how you're feeling right now. How *are* you feeling right now?" She looked at each one of us in turn.

There was a long pause. Then I said, "When did it actually happen?"

Mrs. Chamber looked grateful that I'd spoken. "Well, I can't be certain because of the time zones, but I believe it was some time late Christmas Eve."

My stomach tightened even though I'd already known the answer.

Mrs. Chamber continued. "There will be a memorial service this week for Ms. Blythe. Perhaps you girls would like to participate in some way. Sing or speak? Some older students who participated in her Parks and Rec camp are putting together a PowerPoint presentation with their collected photos."

CJ said, "We never got any photos of Coach Nola because we hadn't played any games or tournaments yet. I would have *so* had my new digital camera there."

That made the twins cry harder.

"Perhaps the team could recite a poem," Mrs. Chamber suggested. "It would be a lovely tribute and might help build a team bond before you move on with your season and new coach."

My head shot up. *New coach?*

Dodie interjected quickly, "I think Summer should speak for us. After all, she was named captain by Coach Nola."

Roxx looked at Dodie and rolled her eyes.

"New coach?" I blurted.

Mrs. Chamber looked taken aback. "Oh, my apologies, Summer. Principal Talbot and I assumed you all knew that Mr. Dirk Rogers generously offered to take over the team."

I scanned the faces of my teammates. No one seemed surprised but me. *Coach Rogers?* My mind started whirling.

Roxx interrupted, "It, like, makes more sense for Karmyn to speak. Summer was only captain for one day, really, if you think about it. Karmyn was captain all last year."

"I could do it." Karmyn sat straighter and perched on the edge of her chair. Looking very serious, she said, "Coach Rogers told me he'll be naming co-captains this year anyway, so I guess it is appropriate for me to do it."

I stared at Karmyn and knew my mouth was open. It was as if I'd lost control of my body parts when I tried to close it. *Coach Rogers!* Karmyn's mother's boyfriend would be coaching us? Karmyn shot me a fake sympathetic look. With the exception of Dodie, all the girls were nodding their heads in agreement. They must all have known about the plans for our team.

Still flustered, Mrs. Chamber glanced around the group

and said, "It is fortuitous that he isn't coaching the varsity boys this year."

Karmyn nodded. "He and my mom are so busy with wedding plans, he decided to take the year off, but our team's schedule is much lighter, so it's perfect! I mean, apart from this sadness…it's perfect. He has tons of higher-level experience."

Faith stopped picking her nail polish long enough to tell Karmyn her stepdad-to-be was great.

Mrs. Chamber added, "Well, I'm sure Ms. Blythe would be pleased that your team will have the benefit of Coach Rogers."

I wanted to yell at Mrs. Chamber. *How do you know what would please Coach Nola? How could she be happy about someone else coaching her team?* And he's marrying Karmyn's mom? And naming co-captains? How did this all happen? He was already making changes, and he hadn't even met us yet! Changes that Karmyn was obviously telling him to make. Why didn't I talk to everyone over the holiday? It was my job, I suddenly realized. Now the team was looking at Karmyn as if she was already full captain again.

"I'll do it!" I blurted. Everyone turned to look at me. "Coach Nola named me captain. It was the last team decision she made before she died. I'll speak at her memorial." Even as I said the words, my knees started quaking.

Karmyn sniffed and said, "But I already said I would."

We stared at each other.

Mrs. Chamber said, "Well that's ideal. You can both contribute. In these circumstances, it can be comforting to have someone with whom you can share the task. I'll ensure you're both added to the program."

Mrs. Chamber uncrossed her legs and padded over to her desk to write herself a sticky note. While she was verifying the correct spelling of my last name, I could tell that Roxx and Karmyn were whispering about me.

I said, "That's okay, Mrs. Chamber. Karmyn did offer first. Just put her name down."

"Are you certain, Summer?" she asked, raising her eyebrows at me.

I nodded my head. "May I go back to class now?"

Mrs. Chamber said if that was what I felt was best, then by all means.

Without looking at Karmyn or any of the other girls, I snatched my backpack and hurried out of Mrs. Chamber's office. Rushing down the hall, it was as if a PA system in my head suddenly switched on. *Attention, Summer Widden: It's not whether you win or lose, it's how you win the game. Well, you didn't win. You lost. You gave up the fight. You let Karmyn beat you in front of all your teammates.*

I opened my locker and rested my head against the top shelf. I wanted to climb inside, close the door behind me and hope that someone would lock me in.

"Summer?"

It was Dodie. I cringed, and the urge to climb into my locker grew stronger. I forced myself to turn to her instead, remembering Mom's insistence I try to be nice. The last thing I needed was to have Dodie tell her mother I'd been mean to her and then have Mrs. Direland report that to Mom at work. I wouldn't want Mom to be in Martha Direland's bad books. That was a scary prospect. Dodie was holding a stack of her own books against her chest, and with her arms still wrapped around them, she bent her head down and pushed her glasses up her nose with her pointer finger.

"Hey, Dodie," I said before turning back into my locker. I pretended to search for a missing assignment.

"I called you over the holidays," she said. "I guess you didn't have a chance to call back."

"Uh, no," I said.

"I was calling to let you know about Coach Rogers taking over the team and all."

"Oh," I said, and took my head out of the locker. "Uh, thanks. That would have been nice to know."

Dodie smiled. Then the smile faded and she looked as if she was going to cry. "It's terrible about Coach Nola, isn't it? I couldn't believe it. I mean, she was such a great person and so cool, and she…well, she…"

At that point, Principal Talbot turned a corner and headed toward us. "Do you girls have a hall pass?" he questioned.

"We just came from Mrs. Chamber's office," Dodie said, looking downright miserable.

"Oh, yes," he said, clearing his throat. "I'm sorry, I know how much the team – all of us – will miss Ms. Blythe."

Dodie and I both looked down at the floor, but not before we spotted a blob of whipped cream and chocolate on his tie. Principal Talbot cleared his throat again and said, "Well, you girls…have…have a nice day."

Dodie took a deep breath as if summoning some inner strength. Then she caught my eye. Trying not to smirk, she ensured Principal Talbot was out of earshot as he hurried off in the opposite direction. We both covered our mouths to stifle a laugh.

"Sorry," Dodie said, "but he just cracks me up. Once he called me into his office and said he wanted to talk to me about my potential in science. The whole time he talked, he ate his entire lunch, even though it was only mid-morning. He kept offering me stuff from his lunch kit, which I declined, and then he concluded by comparing me to Einstein. How weird is that?"

"Well, you are pretty smart," I said.

"Thanks, Summer, but I do have perspective. And believe it or not, I know I can't play basketball very well, but I love it so much, maybe because the plays are practically scientific – mathematical, anyway – if you think about them." Dodie stopped just long enough to take a breath. "The way you run them over and over in a set pattern. When Coach used to draw them on the chalkboard, they looked just like scientific formulas or algebra or something… If only she hadn't died."

"Yeah," I said. "I know."

"It will never be the same without her. I guess all we can do is continue to be a team and see what happens. But you should know, Summer, that I think you are the best choice for captain, too."

I grabbed my binder out of my locker. "Well...thanks, Dodie, but I don't think anyone else agrees." The minute I said it, I regretted it. I didn't want Dodie's sympathy. I didn't even want her on my side. I didn't want to discuss any of this with her. That would ensure that Karmyn and the others would reject me even more. I slammed my locker door a little harder than I intended.

Dodie winced at the bang, then said, "Coach Nola was the one who named you captain, Summer. Fact, not factoid. Coach Nola. I think you should remember it." And with that, she turned and was gone.

CHAPTER EIGHT

I came down with a flu bug on the day of Coach Nola's memorial service, and Mom wouldn't let me attend. "You'll just be spreading those germs, coughing and sneezing through the entire service." I spent the day thinking of her anyway. About how she would demonstrate drills and make them look so easy, but then if we couldn't catch on, she'd break them down into her "mini-me steps" until everyone could manage to get through. About how she would yell, "Yeah, yeah, go, go, go," whenever one of us really did well. She made a point of yelling that for each one of us at least once at every practice. She must have kept a tally in her head, and it didn't seem to matter if it was Karmyn with a steal, a fake and then a fade-away jump-shot, or Dodie just getting her footwork right on a basic layup. Coach gave each of us the same amount of enthusiasm. I still couldn't believe that she wouldn't be there when I walked into the gym for our first practice.

But she wasn't there. Her absence was as conspicuous as the hollow echo of the empty gymnasium when the day finally arrived. Dodie, Val and I were the first three people into the change room after classes. Val, who didn't like to change in front of anyone because of her weight, went into the bathroom stall to dress. Dodie came and sat beside me and laced up her new basketball shoes.

"Are you feeling better?" she asked.

"Yeah, pretty much."

Then she whispered, "You should know that Karmyn's

speech was gag-me-with-a-spoon sickly sweet. She really didn't talk about Coach Nola at all. She read some kind of Hallmark card poem. I don't think Karmyn even liked her."

Val called out from the bathroom stall, "Dodie, I can hear you. And first of all, you're right, but secondly, you'd better not talk about her here in case she comes in."

Dodie looked at me. One part of me wanted to tell Dodie that I appreciated her support, but the other part of me knew that it was too risky. I tried to sound positive when I said, "You know, I'm sure that Karmyn was still upset about the last practice, but things would be different if Coach Nola was here today. It all would have worked out with everyone."

As if on cue, Karmyn, followed by Roxx, barged in.

Roxx said, "They *are* here. It figures."

Karmyn nodded and looked at us as if we were complete idiots. "Practice is cancelled. Didn't you hear the announcement?"

We shook our heads. Val moaned from the bathroom stall. "I just changed," she complained.

"Well, like, unchange," said Roxx, and then mouthed to Karmyn, "if it won't exhaust you."

Karmyn laughed.

I felt sick inside. I needed to play basketball again. I had to know if I *could* play basketball without Coach Nola. And it was becoming obvious that without her influence, Karmyn and Roxx were letting their mean sides out. They didn't have to worry any longer about Coach Nola disapproving of their rude or negative attitudes.

"Why is it cancelled?" Dodie asked.

"Dirk can't make it today. Coach Rogers, I mean," Karmyn replied.

"I thought this was the time he picked!" Dodie said, kicking off her new basketball shoes.

"Why are you worried about it, Dodie? It's not like it will make any difference to you," Karmyn said.

Roxx added, "Neither will your new shoes." She snatched them off the change room floor. "How much did your mommy pay for these, anyway?" She started to put them on her own feet.

I should have said something at that point, but instead, I turned my back to everyone and started to unlace my own basketball shoes, careful to put them right into my bag.

At that moment, the change room door swung open, and CJ and Faith came in with their gear bags.

"You didn't hear, either?" Karmyn said. "No practice, tonight."

"Oh, thank goodness," CJ said. "Night off. Par-tay!"

Faith did a little dance with her arms circling her head.

"What kind of party?" Roxx asked.

"Oh, I don't know," CJ said. "We'll probably just go hang at my house. Do our nails and hair, or something."

"Yeah, and we won't be sweaty," Faith added. "Maybe we wouldn't have been sweaty anyway, though. Depends on whether your step-dad is a beast like Coach Nola or not."

"I'm sure he'll run us pretty hard," said Karmyn with a hint of pride.

"Yuck," said Faith.

I finally spoke. "Well, we won't get any better if Coach Rogers doesn't make us work hard. Think of everything we learned from Coach Nola since last year!"

"Yeah, I know she was hard on us," CJ said unexpectedly, "but I miss her."

Faith relented as soon as CJ spoke. "Yeah, I'd give anything to have her back."

Dodie said, "Me, too. I'd just like to talk to her again."

Everyone acted as if Dodie hadn't spoken, except Roxx, who was still lacing Dodie's shoes on her own feet. She sat down next to Dodie and smirked into her face. "You'd like to talk to Coach Nola? I could probably arrange that, you know?"

Dodie narrowed her eyes but didn't respond. She looked

down at her new shoes and her jaw tightened.

"Upstairs in my attic," Roxx continued, "we have a table that was used for séances by my great-grandmother. It's definitely, like, cursed or something. You can tell whenever you go near it. Once, my mom put it in our garage sale, and when she turned around after pricing it, she tripped on this old pile of record albums and broke her ankle. Garage sale cancelled. When she came home from the emergency room, the price tag from the table had disappeared, but no one in our family had touched it. Table returned to the attic! Wh-oo-oo-oo!" she said, wailing like a ghost and wiggling her fingers in Dodie's face.

Faith squealed, "Get out of here! For real?"

"Yeah, for real," Roxx answered.

"Let's have a séance," Karmyn said.

CJ and Faith high-fived her. "Yeah! Let's!"

"Let's not," said Val, who had finally come out of the bathroom stall in her street clothes.

"Are you scared, Val?" Roxx said, sneering.

I answered for her. "Well paranormal stuff is scary." I thought about Christmas Eve and the terrible panicky feeling I'd had. I'd been trying not to think about it. About how I knew something dreadful had happened before we received the news.

Roxx said, still sneering, "Well, scaredy-cats like Val and Summer aren't invited anyway."

"Yes, they are," Karmyn said. "We're a team, aren't we?" She looked around, and her mouth twitched with a triumphant little smile. "Anyone who doesn't come and be part of the séance isn't on the team." She flipped her long red hair over one shoulder and started running her fingers through it like a comb.

Val said, "But Trish and Tracy aren't even here."

Roxx shrugged. "I can text them." She reached into her pocket and waved what must have been her Christmas present in the air. "We'll meet them on the way to my place. Let's go. No one's parents expect them home for a couple of hours anyway. And my parents always work late."

Dodie said, "How did we go from having a cancelled basketball practice to holding a séance? Summer's right. We should all work on our ball handling or something useful. And I'd like my shoes back now, Roxx."

"Why shouldn't we hold a séance?" Karmyn demanded.

"Well..." Dodie turned to look at Karmyn. She adjusted her glasses before she continued. "Well, first off, it seems rather disrespectful, and secondly, it's a major waste of time. Ghosts don't exist."

Roxx stood and jogged on the spot in Dodie's shoes. "Look, Dodie, if you don't want to come, that's no problem for the rest of us."

Roxx was daring Dodie to say she wasn't coming, so they could feel justified in convincing Coach Rogers to kick her off the team. I knew I should have defended Dodie at that moment. She had been improving with Coach Nola's instruction, and she always tried hard. She didn't deserve the constant put-downs.

Dodie was unfazed. "And thirdly, if I am mistaken, and ghosts actually do exist, then none of us know what we're messing with." Dodie turned to me and said, "Summer you're captain. Are you going to do this?"

"I...I..." All I could do was stammer at first, then I found my voice. "Maybe it would make us feel better if we could contact her. Maybe her spirit wants to be with us." It was the only lame thing I could think of to say. I didn't believe it. I knew that Dodie didn't believe me, but Karmyn and Roxx were more than ready to exclude me as well. To say we shouldn't do it was too risky.

Dodie sighed and said, "Okay, then, if Summer says we're doing it, I'm in."

"Me, too," said Val.

Faith squealed again. “Ohmygod, this is going to be so unbelievable!”

I said, “Now give Dodie back her shoes, Roxx.”

“Oh, fine,” Roxx said. She proceeded to kick them off without untying the laces, sending them across the room. Then she grabbed my bag and yanked my new basketball out of it.

“Oooh, Santa brought el capitano a new ball,” Roxx said.

Karmyn put her hands up for a pass. “Let’s see it.”

Roxx passed it across the change room. Karmyn dribbled it a few times and passed it back to Roxx. “Sweet ball! This should be our game ball, don’t you think, Roxx?”

“Yeah, maybe you should take it home and get Dirk to check it out,” Roxx agreed.

I raised my hand. “Okay, pass my ball back, please.”

Karmyn and Roxx started a little game of keep-away in the change room. Just as I was close enough to cut off Karmyn’s pass, she faked one off to my side. As I looked over to see where Roxx was, Karmyn yelled “Think fast!” and drilled the ball at me. It nailed me in the side of the head, and after a burst of psychedelic red, yellow and blue, the room looked a little grey.

Roxx burst out laughing. “Way to catch…with your face!”

This sent Karmyn, CJ and Faith into a hyena frenzy of laughter, but Dodie grabbed my ball and asked if I was all right.

“Yeah,” I said. “No problem.” I couldn’t tell what was stinging more – the side of my face or the tears I was trying desperately to keep from falling.

CHAPTER NINE

"Leave your bags and stuff here," Roxx instructed. She was standing at the bottom of her attic staircase, holding a candelabrum with three lit candles on it. "The wiring in the attic hasn't been redone, so I'm not allowed to turn on the lights up there."

The stairs that led to the attic were so narrow that we had to ascend single file. I held tightly to the rickety handrail to keep from slipping on the worn bare wood under our sock feet. The candles offered only the slightest of illumination and made our shadows flicker on the wall, which was covered in century-old wallpaper. I knew my dad would have had an electrical inspector out to condemn the place if he were with us. I was tempted to turn tail and run home to tell him, but Val was blocking my escape. She was huddled close behind me, voicing serious second thoughts; I think she only agreed to continue when she realized she was too afraid to be left alone on the first floor, or worse, walk home in the dark by herself.

We crowded together at the top of the stairs. The attic was warm and close. It smelled of dust tinged with mothballs. Roxx traipsed across the floor, grabbed the corner of a white sheet and yanked it off a large round table. As she did so, the sudden movement of air extinguished two of the candles. The remaining flame spit and fought for its life. The twins – who'd been keen to join us when Roxx texted them – screamed in perfect unison. CJ and Faith turned as if to plunge back down the stairs. The rest of us huddled closer together. Roxx laughed, but there was an unnatural, high-pitched strain to it. Only Karmyn seemed unfazed. She started gathering stray chairs and assorted boxes for us to sit on. She ordered me to help her move an old steamer trunk, which she declared would seat at least two. As I strained to push the trunk, the side of my head where the basketball had hit me pulsed and ached.

Roxx relit the two snuffed candles and set the candelabrum in the middle of the table. "Okay, gather around," she said.

CJ, chewing on her fingernail polish, said, "I've only seen séances on TV. What are we supposed to do next?"

Roxx said, "Everyone has to sit down and join hands."

"We don't do anything before that?" CJ asked. "Doesn't everyone have to declare something…like we believe in the spirit world? Don't we swear never to tell anyone what happens tonight?"

Karmyn slapped the palm of her hand on the table, which made everyone jump. "Stop babbling, CJ. If I didn't know better, I'd say you were stalling because now *you're* scared."

CJ cleared her throat and shook her head vehemently.

"We're not scared, Karmyn," Faith said.

Val whispered, "I am."

Trish reached for her sister's hand, and Tracy said, "This is amazing. Our mom gets her tea leaves read every month in a strange little café in Winnipeg. Madam always sees doubles of things in Mom's cup, but Mom has never told her she has twins."

Roxx cut in. "Okay, focus! Just join hands. My great-grandmother was a medium at this very table."

Although no one had been willing to join hands in Mrs. Chamber's office, everyone reached out at the table. I took a hold of Faith's hand, and Dodie clasped my other one. The second all our hands were joined, a current seemed to buzz around the table through us. I fought not to squeeze Dodie's and Faith's fingers.

Roxx closed her eyes and began in a monotone. "Oh, spirit

of our recently departed coach, Nola Blythe…"

CJ and Faith giggled nervously.

Karmyn hissed, "You two are out if you can't control yourselves. Everyone has to concentrate on Coach Nola."

I wasn't so sure I wanted to do that. The whole thing was too creepy. Besides, I'd worked hard to stop the angry ache inside me whenever I thought about her death. Now I was mad at myself for actually participating.

Roxx spoke. "Everyone, concentrate on the last day we saw Coach Nola. Everyone think the same thoughts."

I tried to fight it, but Coach's words came rushing back to me…*I'm naming Summer our captain for this season. Look for her leadership in the new year.* The moment the words resurfaced, the strange wave of emptiness that I'd felt on the night of her plane crash surged inside me. I had the sudden sensation I was standing on a high cliff that was about to crumble beneath me and wash out to sea. I tried to imagine Coach's face instead, but I couldn't recall exactly what she looked like any more. I'd get a flash of her dark eyes and then a memory of her smile, but I couldn't seem to hold the image of her together.

After a short silence, Roxx continued. "We hail you from your realm. We summon you, Coach Nola, to speak with us… guide us. Tell us what we must do to win the Provincial Championship."

I snuck a look around the table. Everyone was staring at Roxx, except for Karmyn, who had her head tilted back as if she was listening to something outside the narrow window behind her, and Val, who had her eyes squeezed shut while her lips moved in some silent prayer.

That was when we heard a low moaning sound.

"What was that?" Val whispered.

"Don't break the circle!" Roxx insisted. "Don't let go of each other's hands."

We all held our breaths before the second moan. It came from Karmyn. She had her head tilted back, her eyes closed and was breathing in short sharp rasps. Then she moaned again.

Roxx whispered, "Coach must be trying to speak through Karmyn."

Val whimpered, but Roxx ignored her. "Speak with us, stay and speak with us."

Karmyn moaned again. Dodie turned to me and tried to catch my eye. I grimaced and she rolled her eyes. Everyone else stared intently at Karmyn. Tracy and Trish had huddled closer together so that not only their hands, but also their shoulders were touching.

In a strangled voice, Karmyn mouthed the barely audible words, "You…must…listen."

"We are listening," Roxx said in a beseeching tone. "What have you come to tell us?"

"You…must…listen. Only one speaks for me…only one speaks for all of you. Listen, and you will win."

Karmyn slumped onto the table and made another low moaning sound.

"What did she mean?" CJ demanded. "Is Karmyn all right?"

Dodie was the first to pull her hands away. As soon as she did, Faith and CJ went straight to Karmyn, who raised her head and looked dazed, as if she didn't recognize any of us.

Roxx said, "Ohmygod, Karmyn. Coach Nola spoke through you. Do you remember any of it?"

Karmyn squinted as if the candlelight was hurting her eyes. She shook her head, still looking dazed.

The twins joined in. "That was awesome!" one of them said.

Dodie muttered under her breath, "Give it up, Karmyn."

"What did you say, Dodie?" Roxx demanded.

"Nothing," Dodie said in a falsetto voice.

The three candles flickered and spat out all at once. The room was pitched into blackness. Screeches pierced the sudden gloom. I felt what must have been Val jump up off of the trunk and clutch at my arm. Someone tipped over a chair and there was another chorus of screaming. As my eyes adjusted, I could see a sliver of light from what I thought must be the staircase, and a pale glow seeping in from the narrow window.

I wanted out of that attic. It was obvious that Karmyn was still trying to regain her position of superiority over the team, and I'd had enough.

I groped my way toward what I thought was the top of the staircase, hoping that I wouldn't miss the railing and go crashing down. The screaming continued behind me, but I was distracted by a strange aroma wafting over me. Had the candles been coconut scented? I reached the edge of the first step and felt a bone-chilling draught. I inched my foot forward, but it slipped over the edge of the top stair and I felt myself teetering. Suspended in air, my arms flailing for a hand-hold – I saw something! At the bottom of the staircase, amid our bags and coats – a filmy, vaporous figure hovered there. As it raised its head, I unexpectedly regained my balance. The face that I hadn't been able to conjure a few moments earlier was staring up at me. Coach Nola. In a flicker, she was gone.

It was more like a muffled howl than a scream, and it took an instant before I realized it was coming from me. The rest of the team ceased their commotion, frozen into silence. I launched myself back toward the group. Roxx struck a match and relit the candles.

"Ohmygod, what was that weird noise?" CJ demanded.

I opened my mouth to speak, but nothing came out. I reached for the twins, who were standing closest to me, but they jumped away.

"What's the matter, Summer?" Trish demanded.

Tracy was even more adamant. "Stop scaring us!"

I closed my eyes, but the face came back to me. The pale visage, the deep, sorrowful eyes. I gulped for air as my heart pounded in my chest. Even though I was afraid, much more powerful emotions were surging through me. Had I seen Coach Nola? Or was it just the slit of light from the second floor cutting through the darkness that made me think I'd seen her? It wasn't like her at all. There was no sparkle in her eyes, no energy, no muscle twitch preparing to burst down the court toward the hoop. It was just a vague, colourless, morose presence.

I said, "I think I saw her."

"What?" The whole team exploded with questions. "What did you see? What do you mean you saw her? Where?"

"At the bottom of the stairs."

Roxx marched straight to the staircase, candelabrum held high. "There's no ghost here," she insisted as she descended to the second floor and turned on a hall light. "Everyone, come down," she called. No one needed to be asked twice.

At Roxx's front door, Karmyn and Roxx started laughing. Roxx said, "We were just kidding around, you guys. We were just trying to have some fun and scare everybody."

Karmyn reengaged her blank look, moaned and then burst out laughing. But even as her laughter trailed off, she shot me a reproachful look.

A tangible wave of relief spread through the team. Everyone joined in the laughter except Val and me.

Dodie chimed in, directing her words at Val. "There are no such things as ghosts coming back from the dead." But even as she finished, Dodie looked at me curiously, raised one eyebrow and frowned.

I nodded my head slowly. "I was just joshing, too! There are no such things as ghosts," I agreed, and tried to join in the laughter. I slid my hand over the side of my face and felt the tender spot where I'd been whacked by the basketball. Maybe I'd been hit harder than I realized.

CHAPTER TEN

The January night sky was clear with just a crescent sliver of moon. I squinted at its narrow light. It seemed unfriendly in the same way a jester's smile can be more menacing than playful. The temperature outside had dropped while we'd been in Roxx's attic. The snow squeaked in protest under my boots. I kept checking over my shoulder to make sure nothing was following me. By the time I reached my house, my fingers and toes were numb with the cold. In my driveway was a small red car I didn't recognize. The last thing I wanted was to be polite to company. I thought of hiding out in the garage for a while, but the night was too cold.

I slipped in through the back door as quietly as possible. I could hear the rattle of dishes and cutlery and Holly directing someone to the cupboard where we kept the paper napkins.

As I unzipped my parka, Holly stuck her head around the corner. "That was quick pick-up… Oh! I thought you were Mom and Dad back with the pizza."

A second later, Holly's boyfriend, Everett, joined us. "Hey Summer, how was practice?" he asked, pushing his longish blond hair back from his face.

I turned away to hang my parka in the closet. "Okay." I breathed on my hands, which were starting to tingle as my blood thawed – partly to warm them, partly to hide the lie on my face.

It was Everett's first visit to our house. It was nice to see him there, but at the same time, if he hadn't been there, I figured

Holly wouldn't be exercising the big sister role. Instead, she would have been working on a college assignment or chatting online and would barely have acknowledged that I'd returned home.

Holly lowered her voice sympathetically and asked, "So, how is the new coach, then?"

"Uh...okay. He just let us sort of scrimmage our first time back and everything." How could I possibly tell anyone what just happened?

When I forced a smile toward the two of them, Holly cocked her head sideways. "You don't look so great, Summer. You're really pale under those cold red cheeks."

"I guess I'm not totally over the flu," I fibbed again. "I'm going to lie down."

"Hey, but Mom and Dad are picking up from Little Italy Eatery for us. Your fave! Extra, extra-large Hawaiian," she said, licking her lips.

I tried to smile. "I might have some later."

Holly frowned and glanced at Everett. I used the opportunity to slip past them and took the stairs to my room two at a time, my gym bag bouncing against my thigh.

"Nice to see you, Everett," I called over my shoulder. I shut my bedroom door, flung my bag into the closet and threw myself face-down on the bed. My head hurt more than I expected when I landed. I shut my eyes, and the face that had looked up the stairs at me suddenly reappeared. I scrunched my eyes tight, tried to squeeze it away, but it remained, stubbornly staring at me. The sad dark eyes didn't recognize me, didn't even really see me. *Who is she looking at, if not me? Who is she looking for?*

I managed to avoid the dinner table altogether by crawling under the covers and pretending I was still not feeling well. I listened to the chatter downstairs. Mom was laughing more than usual; I imagined that meant she really liked Everett. And Dad found some of his old jazz cassettes to entertain him. I wanted to go and join them so that I could stop thinking about the séance and the ghostly figure, but at the same time, I had to try to understand it – and the strange connection on Christmas Eve.

A couple of hours later, after I heard Everett's car leave the driveway, there was a soft knock at my door and Dad stuck his head in.

"You're still awake?" he asked.

"Uh…yeah," I said.

"So, Holly said your practice went okay."

"Yeah."

"What did you think of Coach Rogers?" he asked and shoved his hands into his pockets.

"Okay, I guess." I was glad for the darkness that hid the colour creeping into my cheeks.

"Hmmm. That's interesting," Dad said in a strange voice.

I was quick to add, "He's not Coach Nola."

"No, but he must be pretty terrific, nevertheless…"

"What do you mean?" I asked.

Dad paused. "Well, I would think it would take a special kind of coach to be in two places at the same time."

I felt the creeping colour surge and flush my entire face and neck. "I…uh, what do you mean?" I repeated, grasping for anything to say.

"I think you do know, Summer," Dad said, and teetered from his heels to his toes, his hands still shoved in his pockets. "Coach Rogers was at a staff meeting at the high school with me, so he couldn't have been running your practice tonight."

"Dad, I…I just didn't want to talk about it. About how hard it's been, waiting for this practice and then Coach Rogers doesn't show and then…and then…"

"Why were you so late if there was no practice?" Dad said, ignoring my gush of words.

"The whole team went to Roxx's house...and we just talked about basketball and stuff."

"There was no need to lie about it, Summer," Dad admonished. "The next time there will be some serious consequences. Just because you're sad about Ms. Blythe doesn't excuse you from proper behaviour, understood?"

I breathed out. "Okay, Dad. Sorry."

He shut my bedroom door behind him without another word. At first I had the urge to drag my desk across the floor to block anyone else from coming in. Then I wanted to shout out *You don't understand anything!* In the next second, I wanted to call Dad back and tell him all about what had happened that evening. But would he believe what I had to say when it sounded like an even bigger lie than the one I'd just told? It wasn't like Dad to deal with these kinds of issues in our house – he usually left that up to Mom. And there was no way I could tell her any of this. How someone with such an eager will to laugh could always be looking for the next catastrophe, I'd never know. The first thing she'd ask is if there was alcohol or drugs at Roxx's house to make me imagine such a thing. She'd follow that closely with did I have one of my fainting episodes? Ever since my growth spurt, the world often went a little grey when I stood up too quickly; Mom explained it as a sudden drop in my blood pressure. In the end, she'd somehow get me to admit that I'd taken a ball to my bean before we left the school and she'd be reluctant to let me play again, I was sure of it.

"Your own teammates did that?" she'd say. "Well, there's no need to put yourself at risk, Summer. You'll just have to find something else to do. How about some volunteer work at the seniors' centre?"

From the closet, I dug my basketball out of my gym bag.

"Traitor," I said to it, holding Spalding at eye level. "You're not supposed to bash my brains out; you're supposed to be on my side!"

Thankfully, Spalding did not respond. It spun between my

fingertips with its cheery, weighted roundness and acted like a ball – nothing more – not a confidante or an enemy. Just a ball. I felt a tiny sense of relief that I might not be going insane after all. The relief was short-lived. I recalled the ghostly face. How the figure had hovered right over our pile of bags and the very ball I held in my hands. I dropped Spalding onto my bed and sat back from it. Might there be some ghostly trace on it? Some spirit residue? If I stared at it long enough, might it rise off the bed and bounce onto the floor? Dodie had been so absolutely positive that there were no such things as ghosts coming back from the dead. But how did she know? How did anyone know? A shiver ran over my skin and down each vertebrae of my back. At the same time, my stomach growled. I hadn't eaten since noon. I wondered if there was any leftover pizza. It took a kind of panicky courage to exit my room and face the bottom of our darkened stairs. I scampered down them and rounded the corner into the kitchen, accompanied by the slight sense that Spalding might come rolling after me. I flicked on the fluorescent fixture above the sink and wished it had a less ghostly glow against the deep winter darkness outside the window. I could see my own reflection in the glass pane. Was that how I'd look if I were a ghost?

There was one pizza slice left in the box, and I forced myself to eat it. It was cold, soggy, and I couldn't stop looking over my shoulder to make sure no one was watching me eat. I stayed at the kitchen table while the pizza formed a lump in my stomach, right below the tight eerie knot that had taken up residence inside me.

CHAPTER ELEVEN

Coach Rogers was not what I had expected. Unreasonably, I'd imagined him to resemble Karmyn, with red hair, even though they weren't related. He hardly had any hair at all, and it wasn't red. What he did have, he combed over the top of his bare head in thin, sandy-coloured strands. This made his eyebrows look bushier. He was one of those middle-aged fit men who you could imagine attending even symphonies in neat, co-ordinated track suits and running shoes. He had a springy, heels-not-required walk that made him look like he was constantly tilted forward. We discovered at his first practice with us that he often smacked the front of his forehead with the lower part of his palm. I wondered if that habit was contributing to his baldness.

He blew his whistle, three shrill blasts. "Okay, girls, well, I can see that you're not used to running this much, so maybe we'll have a little fun game here, eh?"

"Oh, Dirk, I mean Coach, can we play Bump, puh-leese?"

I had never seen Karmyn act quite so sickly sweet before.

"Good idea," Coach Rogers responded. "Does everyone know how to play Bump?"

We all nodded, eager for one of our favourite games.

"Good, I'll run over it once again, just in case."

Dodie slid me a sideways glance and heaved a sigh. I tried not to respond so that Coach Rogers wouldn't notice. I wasn't sure if Dodie was upset with him or worried about having to shoot free throws.

"Here's the idea," Coach Rogers explained. "You line up at the foul line. The first person shoots. If she scores, she runs to the back of the line, and the next girl throws. If the first girl misses, she has to retrieve her ball and shoot from wherever she rebounds it. She shoots until she sinks one, unless the girl behind her can score first. The second girl shoots from the foul line as soon as the first girl has shot from there. You don't wait, understand? Now, if the second girl should happen to sink her ball before the first girl does, then the first girl has to go sit down. She's out. Kaput! The second girl runs to the back of the line and so on and so forth. Got that?"

Dodie piped in. "We played this before with Coach Nola."

Dead silence. Karmyn and Roxx exchanged looks. A slight smirk, almost undetectable, jumped from one to the other. Val bit her lip. I held my breath. Since the séance, no one had dared speak Coach Nola's name, and no one had talked about what had happened in Roxx's attic. *Surreal*, that's how it felt to me, since those two things seemed to be all I could think about.

Coach Rogers popped his whistle in his mouth and chewed on it. "What's your name?" he asked Dodie, talking around the plastic.

"Dodie."

"Your last name?"

"Direland."

"Okay, you go first, then."

Dodie looked embarrassed. She always stood near the back of the line during Bump so that it looked like she was in the game a little longer.

She sidled to the foul line, placing her toes well back from the mark on the floor.

"Move to the line," Coach Rogers barked.

Dodie looked at him and inched forward a bit.

"Right up!" he insisted.

Dodie stood with her toes almost touching the line and

threw the ball. Her shot was way short of the rim, and upon her release, she landed well in front of the foul line.

"You can't cross the line. Your feet don't leave the floor on a free throw! And if they do, you make sure you go straight up and come straight back down!" Coach Rogers bellowed.

Dodie stood where she was and looked at him.

In the meantime, Karmyn shot from behind her and sank her first throw.

"You're out, Dodie!" Roxx said with a spark of glee in her voice.

Dodie retrieved her ball and went to sit on the sideline. Coach Rogers pivoted away from her and smacked the front of his forehead.

Dodie wrapped her arms around her knees and her ball and didn't cheer from the sideline like she normally would have.

It came down to Karmyn and me for the final two. I couldn't help but glance over at Dodie to see if she was okay. It was bad enough that the girls mistreated her; now it appeared Coach Rogers had taken up the cause. As I rebounded a third time, Karmyn put up a second shot layup and knocked me out.

Coach Rogers gave his step-daughter-to-be a high five. Karmyn beamed.

He blew his whistle again. "Okay, girls, let's have a little scrimmage. How many are we?" He counted heads. "Ah, odd number. Okay we'll do a little four-on-four then. And what's your name again?"

"Dodie."

"Your last name?"

"Direland."

"Okay, then, *Dire Straits*, you'll be off to start. Maybe you can practise free throws from the side basket there – if you stay out of the way."

Dodie didn't look at anyone. She went straight to the side basket and stood with her back to us and her ball at her side.

As Coach Rogers began to divide us into two teams, I raised my hand.

"What's your name?"

"Summer," I answered.

"Your last name!" he repeated, exasperated.

"Widden," I answered, and then swallowed before I added, "Whenever we had an odd number, Coach Nola would play on the short-handed team, so that everyone was able to practise together."

Coach Rogers chewed on his whistle again. His bare forehead creased and flushed. "Well, that probably worked fairly well for Ms. Blythe, seeing as she was a girl. Now, if I was to play on the short-handed team there would be a lopsided advantage. Don't you think, *Withering Heights?*"

I breathed in. *Coach Nola would whip your butt one-on-one if she were still alive.* Swallowing those words, I said, "Well, you could adjust to play at our level."

Coach Rogers guffawed and the whistle flew out of his mouth. "Ah, just play down, eh? I think my plan will work better." He smiled so hard, I thought his lips might disappear completely, but it wasn't a smile you'd want turned your way. He continued. "Our job, your job, everyone's job on this team is to move forward from here."

Dodie had turned around to listen to his response. After he finished, she took careful aim, bent her knees like Coach Nola had taught her, and sank her first free throw. She turned around in triumph and I gave her a thumbs-up, hoping no one else saw.

For the next thirty minutes, we scrimmaged hard, with only a couple of water breaks. It felt good to be back on the court. So much of what Coach Nola had taught us came flooding back. I faked once from the top of the key and then drove in past CJ for a layup. It was the first time I'd managed to do it in a scrimmage situation, even though Coach Nola had run it over and over with me during drills. *Beat your opponent to the hoop, Summer. If she's there with you, then either run faster or run smarter, but beat her.*

It wasn't until we'd hit the change room and I was in my street gear that I realized Dodie had not been subbed in. She had been left on the sideline, shooting free throws the entire time. Val had called for a sub at one point, and Coach Rogers told her to wait one more minute until the water break. After the break, he sent Val back in.

I looked around the room. "Where's Dodie?" I muttered.

I went around the corner and checked the shower area for her, but she was gone.

When I turned around, Karmyn stood right in front of me. "Summer, we should talk."

"Sure," I said, uncertain about why she would follow me.

"Listen, we need you on the floor playing, you know?"

I didn't know what sort of response she expected. I could feel myself smiling sheepishly.

"So, like, some advice, okay? First, Dirk doesn't waste his time with lost causes. I think you know who I mean. And second, the one thing he really hates is when a player tells him about the way Coach so-and-so does stuff. That really pisses him off. I'm only telling you this because we can't afford to have you on the bench, unlike a few others around here."

At that point, Roxx came around the corner and piped up, "Hang with losers and you are one, Summer."

Karmyn raised her hand, and Roxx stopped talking. "Dirk said Nola Blythe should never have raised our hopes about the Provincial Final, but he also said now that he's taking over the team, we stand a realistic chance. He's going to try and make it happen."

The criticism of Coach Nola plunged like a dagger deep into my stomach. There was a steadily increasing over-crowding problem happening down there. Soon there'd be no room for food if these bad feelings didn't stop swelling inside me.

Karmyn must have sensed my anger. She checked over her

shoulder to see if Roxx was still there. Roxx was putting her jacket on in the other room. Karmyn lowered her voice and said, "Dirk is willing to keep you as co-captain, Summer, because I told him what a good player you are. Don't blow your chance. Nola Blythe would never have wanted you to blow your chance." She raised her eyebrows at me, and her green eyes darkened.

I shrugged a little and nodded even less. Karmyn frowned at me.

I faltered, felt as if I was slipping on ice. I had to say something to keep her from stomping off. "Hey, thanks, Karmyn."

Karmyn smiled at me. She seemed satisfied. "Let's go, Roxx," she called out, then turned back, and from behind her hand, she said, "Dodie is only going to drag us down, Summer. I know you want this team to make it to the big win, so stop feeling sorry for Dodo-bird. Some people just aren't meant to be out there. That's not our fault."

A few minutes later, I went and stood alone in the gym. Everyone else had vacated. I took deep breaths of the familiar gym air, laden with sweat and energy, defeat and triumph. Karmyn's words still held me off balance. They were like the icy January roads outside. The faster you tried to steer away from them, the more you stayed in one spot, spinning your tires. You couldn't ignore the ice underneath if you wanted to negotiate forward. It seemed to me that I'd been stuck in some kind of weird limbo ever since Coach Nola had died. Weird enough that I actually thought I'd been awakened by her crash and had seen her ghost. Weird enough that I'd actually started to feel sorry for Dodie because Coach wasn't there to say "Yeah, yeah, go, go, go!" I hadn't even liked Dodie at the start of the season, and I wasn't sure I'd changed my mind about her, despite Mom insisting I should. I felt thankful for her support, but also guilty about it. If I couldn't be nice in return, I shouldn't accept the support.

I sat down in the middle of the court, in the jump-ball area. I traced my finger in a big circle around me, following the painted lines over and over, and I tried to understand all the conflicting feelings inside me. If Nola Blythe were still alive, she would be coaching us to win Provincials. That was her plan. And if that was her plan, then the new year would have brought major change to our team anyway, wouldn't it? She would have had to make the right choice and leave Dodie on the sidelines more and more to allow the rest of us to do our job on the court. Wouldn't she?

The words I hadn't repeated now for several weeks came flooding back. *It's not whether you win or lose, it's how you win the game.* Her words finally made sense. You had to be prepared to do what it takes to win. That's how you win the game.

I stopped tracing the circle and I felt resolve harden inside me. At the same moment, a chilly draught swept over my shoulders. I checked behind me to see if someone had just opened the gym doors. They were shut tight. When I turned my head, I caught a whiff of something coconut-y, and then, overriding the silence of the gym, came a low throbbing hum. I jumped to my feet, grabbed my bag to run, but I couldn't move. There she was! Sitting on the bottom row of the bleachers! Coach Nola! Or at least a figure that resembled her in the same way the thing at the bottom of the attic stairs resembled her. The figure raised her arm as if she were about to point at me, but her wrist snapped and the arm hung there as if she'd just shot a free throw from the line. Her eyes seemed to be looking right through me instead of at me.

I shrieked. I know I did because I heard my voice. But it seemed as if the sound couldn't have originated from inside of me. A moment later, the night custodian, Mr. Portney, came running into the gym, brandishing a wide mop.

He stopped abruptly when he saw me standing there. "Hey," he said. "Students aren't allowed in the gym without supervision."

I pointed to the bleachers. My mouth opened, but I couldn't speak.

He narrowed his eyes toward where I was pointing. Coach Nola's arm still hung in the air.

He said, "Don't try to be funny, kid. Go on, get home. Next time I catch you in here alone, I'll report you to the principal."

I clutched my sports bag to my chest, squeezed my eyes into narrow slits so I wouldn't have to see her any more, and ran.

CHAPTER TWELVE

"Please, Dodie, you have to come back to the school with me!" I panted, standing outside her back door.

"What? Why? Summer, I've got a ton of homework and it's my night for dishes." She squinted at me through her glasses.

My chest heaved, and the frigid January air slashed my lungs. I bent over for a minute, trying to catch my breath.

"Are you okay?" Dodie asked. "Why don't you come inside for a minute?"

I shook my head, refusing to go inside, even though my fingertips were numb from the cold. It was the kind of night when chimney smoke rises straight up and your own breath forms frost on the tiny hairs of your face. My teeth started to chatter as I stood outside Dodie's back door, maybe from the cold, maybe from what I'd just seen.

"Dodie, if I help you with your dishes, will you please come?" I clamped my jaw down to try to stop the chattering. I breathed through my nose and felt the cold sting right into my eyeballs. I coughed and swallowed hard. "Look, I wanted to tell you that what Coach Rogers did to you at practice was terrible. You should have been subbed in, okay? I looked for you after practice, but you'd already left."

"I had lots of homework," Dodie said, her voice flat as she looked away from me and down at her feet.

My resolve against Dodie and her lack of basketball skills was crumbling. I needed to talk to someone about what I'd just seen. "Look," I continued. "Karmyn said Coach Rogers gets furious when players talk about other coaches, so maybe don't mention…don't mention…well, you know… Dodie, listen, I think I saw her in the gym on the bleachers."

"Karmyn?"

"No! I think I saw Coach Nola." I practically shouted it.

Dodie's eyes widened, and she looked over her shoulder. She whispered, "Summer, you'd better come in."

From the living room, I heard Mrs. Direland call, "Who's at the door, Dodie?"

"It's Summer. She forgot some of her homework assignments at school, and she needs some help." Dodie disappeared around the corner for a moment and then came back carrying her ski jacket.

Her mother called after her, "You understand I'm not doing your job for you?"

Dodie called back, shoving her arms into her jacket sleeves, "Don't worry, I'll do the dishes as soon as I get back."

Once we were outside, Dodie said, "Summer, what are you talking about?"

I started in the direction of the school and said, "Dodie, I know this sounds way crazy, but we have to go back to the gym. Remember the other night in Roxx's attic, when I screamed? Well, I thought I saw Coach Nola at the bottom of the stairs. It was just like this fleeting glimpse, but tonight, I… I saw her. She was sitting on the bleachers and she raised her arm as if she was shooting a basketball. But it's not really like her. I mean she doesn't smile, and her eyes look as if they don't see anything. I don't know if she sees me or if she's ignoring me or if she's trying to tell me something but can't speak."

"Summer, slow down!"

I was practically sprinting again, but my mouth seemed to be running faster.

Dodie caught hold of my sports bag and pulled me to a stop. "Are you saying that you're seeing Coach Nola's ghost?"

I nodded. "Yeah, I guess it's like her ghost." I started walking quickly again, dragging Dodie with me.

Dodie let go of my bag and scrambled to keep pace. Her breath came out in frosty bursts. "Summer, I don't believe for one instant that dead people crawl out of their graves and go haunting."

"Well, it's not like I spend my days thinking about ghosts either, Dodie. About the only time I was ever scared of ghosts was once at summer camp when we told stories around the campfire."

Dodie gestured in the cold air with her mitten-covered hands. "It's probably just that you were thinking so much about her. I mean, first the séance, and then our actual first practice. You can't deny she was front and centre on your mind both times. And all it would take would be something odd about the lighting – maybe one of the gym bulbs burned out, and Roxx's attic was so dark – and then all of a sudden, you thought you were seeing her. I'm sure that's all it was, Summer. I mean, we're all still grieving and you weren't even able to attend the memorial service, so it's like you've had no...what's that called? Closure!"

We reached the school. The windowless gym was nearest to where we stood in the parking lot. Ghosts could pass through brick walls. I held my breath a moment, wondering if she would float out toward us.

"So, now what?" Dodie asked. "It looks as if the custodian is the only one here. She nodded in the direction of a single truck parked closest to the doors, then tucked her chin into the collar of her ski jacket to try to keep warm. "Will the school even be unlocked?"

"You know that single door exit by the big refuse bins? I think that's open in the evenings."

We made our way around to the side of the school. It was dark except for the single bulb over the door. I pulled on the handle, and the door opened a smidgen. I looked at Dodie.

"Should we go in?" I whispered.

Dodie nodded impatiently.

I opened the door a crack wider and checked to make sure Mr. Portney wasn't around. There was nothing but a cart with garbage cans stacked on it and some broken chairs under the stairwell. I opened the door even wider. Dodie and I both took a look before we entered. The gym was down a short hall and we dashed for it. The gym doors were closed. My heart sank. What if they were locked? Dodie barged ahead of me and pressed the latch very carefully so it wouldn't make a lot of noise. She opened the gym door and we let it shut just as quietly behind us.

The gym lights had been dimmed. The red exit signs glowed in three different corners of the room, and two other lights shone beside each of the exits. The bleachers were in deep shadow and although I did not want to look there, my eyes darted quickly down the row of them despite myself. Nothing.

I pointed and whispered, "That's where I saw her."

Dodie started off across the gym floor. At centre court, she stopped and surveyed the room. I joined her, sat down and started to trace the jump-ball circle with my fingers. "This is what I was doing when I saw her," I whispered again.

"I don't see anything," Dodie whispered back.

"Me neither," I said and sighed, partly out of relief and partly out of frustration. What had I seen? Was it real or was I just imagining things?

"Why were you sitting on the floor here?" Dodie asked.

"I don't know. I was just thinking really hard about stuff. Like the Provincials and everything. And Coach Rogers, and the way the other girls sometimes act, and I don't know…" I finished with a lie. I couldn't tell Dodie everything Karmyn and Roxx had said about losers.

"So you weren't thinking about Coach at all when she supposedly appeared?"

"Yeah, I was. Right before she appeared," I said, glad to change the subject. "I was absolutely thinking about her and what she'd said to me the last time I saw her."

"But no one else saw what you saw at Roxx's, and you were alone here?" Dodie continued.

"Actually, Mr. Portney came in and I pointed at her. He looked, but he obviously didn't see anything. He just told me to get out." I stood suddenly. "Maybe we should get out. I just remembered that he said if he caught me in here again without supervision, he'd report me."

Dodie waved her hand as if she couldn't care less about Mr. Portney's warning. "Two different places, but you're the common factor. Supposing there was such a thing as ghosts, which, as I said, I don't believe. Why you? Why around our team and on the court?" Dodie puzzled. "I saw a ghost movie once that said ghosts haunted because they had unfinished business."

"Well, how do we know she's not appearing other places, too?" I asked.

While Dodie seemed to weigh that thought, I glanced toward the bleachers again. Nothing.

I said, almost sadly, "We're both thinking about her now, and she's not here."

Dodie looked around the gym again. She shrugged. "Maybe she's in the gym office."

I frowned. I wasn't sure if Dodie was making fun of me or not.

"Seriously," she said.

"Well, we can't get in there. And what do you think? She's hiding in there, waiting for the perfect moment to float out and scare the heck out of us?" Now I felt annoyed and stupid. Even in the eerie dimmed light, I was starting to think that I hadn't seen anything.

"Let's check the office," Dodie said, as if she suddenly had a hunch.

"Dodie!" I exclaimed. "What for?"

She was across the room in a flash, trying the doorknob. Locked. Dodie stamped her foot. "I just remember after every practice, she used to go into the gym office. Sometimes she'd shower, but afterward, she would always sit down and make notes about the session. Remember? I used to think she was a very studious coach. And that's the image I always have of her when I think of her – not out on the court, but bent over her notes at the desk."

"The last time she talked to me," I confirmed as if Dodie might be on to something, "she was standing right here in the doorway."

Suddenly we heard water running. I grabbed Dodie's hand and tried to pull her away from the door.

She stood her ground, staring me down, calming me with her fixed gaze. "Do you have your student card in your bag?" she asked in an almost inaudible whisper.

"Yeah. Why?" I said, my heart pounding inside my coat.

Dodie held out her palm.

I rummaged in the outside pocket of my sports bag and pulled out my student card.

Dodie took it and wedged it between the office door and the frame, right at the latch. It slid deeper, and Dodie grabbed the knob and pushed. The door swung open. We stood on the threshold peering into the darkness, holding our breaths. We could still hear water running, now even more loudly, but we couldn't tell if it was coming from the shower in the back of the gym office or not.

"Do you think she's back there?" I asked out loud.

Dodie pressed her glasses against her face and squinted harder into the darkness.

Suddenly the sound stopped. We both breathed out.

There was a loud shout from behind us! "Hey, you two!"

We whirled around to see Mr. Portney pushing a bucket with a string mop out of the boys' change room.

He dropped the mop and hurried toward us as fast as his old bow legs could carry him. "What the hey are you doing here?" He recognized me and said, "I thought I already kicked you out of here once tonight! What are you up to? Hey? Answer!"

Without missing a beat, Dodie said, "She forgot her ball here tonight. It was a Christmas present, and her parents will ground her if she doesn't bring it home. We were just trying to get the equipment room key to get her ball out. You mustn't have pulled this door tight, because it wasn't locked."

Mr. Portney looked as if he didn't believe Dodie for an instant. "What're your names?" he demanded.

Again, Dodie answered. "I'm Krystal Ball, and she's Winter Day."

"There are no kids with the last name of *Day* in this whole friggin' community. That much I know. You girls come on down to the main office with me. We'll make some phone calls."

"Okay," Dodie said, and she waited for Mr. Portney to start pushing his bucket ahead of him toward the main office hallway. Quick as a blink, she grabbed my hand and yanked me in the opposite direction toward the doors we'd just entered by.

In a flash, "Krystal Ball" and I were running out of the school as if we'd just seen a ghost.

CHAPTER THIRTEEN

"Detentions for a week?" Mom demanded. She was still wearing her mint-coloured nurse's uniform and hadn't even taken the time to remove the stethoscope from around her neck. She was trying to keep her voice calm but was failing. That more or less set the tone for the rest of her tirade. "How embarrassing to have the principal call me at work! Thank goodness they didn't call your father. Can you imagine? He works in the school division, Summer. His daughter should not be giving grief to custodians and principals. Surely you understand that? Holly never did anything like this. And what about poor Dodie? I have to face her mother at work, too. Thank goodness you at least admitted it was entirely your fault, and Dodie wasn't punished."

Dad removed his glasses and rubbed his brow with the back of his hand. "Olivia," he cautioned. In response, Mom sank onto the sofa and clamped her jaw shut to keep from saying more.

Dad placed his glasses low on his nose and, peering over them, said, "Summer, you're very fortunate that administration didn't choose to suspend your extra-curricular activities and kick you off the basketball team."

I wanted to tell them that it was Dodie who broke into the gym office and it was Dodie's idea to run, but I sensed that would somehow land me in deeper trouble. Besides, I had to take the responsibility for Dodie being there in the first place. Or perhaps Coach Nola should be taking responsibility! I shook my head. *She's dead, Summer*, I reminded myself. *Her ghost then!* There, I finally admitted it in my own head. *It was her ghost I saw in the gym. It had to be.* The skin on my neck tingled, and my spine felt as if a trickle of ice water ran down it.

Mom interrupted my thoughts. "Summer, you're not paying the slightest attention to what we're saying to you, are you?" She stood again and said, "Paul, she's ignoring our concerns!"

I tried to refocus on Mom and Dad. I bowed my head and mumbled, "Look, I'm sorry. We shouldn't have gone back for my ball, but I didn't want to risk it not being there in the morning."

Running back to Dodie's house that night, we'd decided in breathless gasps to stick to the forgotten ball story, adding the little detail that we'd found it in the gym office.

Mr. Portney, the custodian, had turned red in the face and told Principal Talbot that we were lying about the ball, but it was obvious that Principal Talbot didn't want to hear anything negative about Dodie Direland. In the end, he actually commended her for trying to help out a friend. I believed that was partly due to the fact that an iced cinnamon bun was sitting beside his telephone and his eyes frequently glanced over at it as if he wanted us all out of his office so he could enjoy his morning coffee break.

When we had finally been sent on our way, Dodie tried to apologize for my detentions. I'd waved off her concerns.

She'd said, "At least they're early-morning detentions and you won't miss practice."

"Yeah," I'd agreed. But the idea of being back in the gym had generated a feeling of unease inside me.

"Summer!" Mom shrieked in exasperation. "I asked you a question."

"Sorry, Mom, I guess I didn't hear you."

Mom and Dad exchanged glances. Mom's eyes grew wide, but Dad cleared his throat and Mom repeated her question. "What do you think your punishment at home should be?"

"No TV for a week?" I offered.

"That's reasonable." Dad jumped in before Mom could decide on something more severe.

Mom stood grim-faced without a hint of laughter in one single pore of her body.

Dad queried, "Don't you think that's fair, Olivia?"

Mom remained staring at me for a moment. Her mouth opened and closed before she finally nodded agreement. Dad put his arm around Mom's shoulders and said, "Settled then."

As if I weren't still sitting in the room, Mom muttered, "I just don't understand what's gotten into her."

At that moment, the front door burst open, and Holly and Everett bounded in. Mom and Dad tried to switch on their most welcoming smiles but obviously didn't quite make the grade.

"What's wrong?" Holly looked from them to me and back again.

Everett put his hand back on the door handle, unsure if he should be making a hasty exit.

Dad answered, "Summer has landed in some trouble at school. Nothing too serious." He tried to reassure everyone.

Holly looked surprised. Everett let go of the door handle and helped Holly shrug out of her jacket.

"Maybe you should head to your room, Summer," Mom said, not looking at me. I could see, as upset as she was, that her request was not just a form of punishment but also a way to save me further embarrassment.

I wasn't halfway up the stairs when Holly asked what had happened. "Holly, maybe we should discuss this…" Mom started, but Dad chose to interject with a full explanation.

In my room, I sat with my ear to the hot air register, where the sound carried the best from the kitchen. My family plus Everett had congregated there.

I heard Everett offer, "Well, I would have done the same in her situation. I would have wanted my ball back."

Holly's sigh was loud enough to hear upstairs. "Don't defend her, Everett. It's like break and enter!"

"Well, she wasn't trying to steal anything," he insisted. "She was just recovering what was hers. My brother and I did something much crazier than that back in junior high to get one of our basketballs back."

"What did you do?" my mother asked, her tone suddenly more relaxed.

He began slowly, drawing everyone's attention in.

I shuffled sideways over the vent so that I could hear better.

"We were playing three-on-three on the outdoor court after school when some skateboarder gang wheeled through our game, grabbed our ball and heaved it onto the flat school roof." He paused there, and then continued. "Baxter and I climbed the dumpster bins and then tried to shimmy up a drain pipe using the brick wall for toe-holds, but we were already fairly tall by then and a little gangly and uncoordinated. We couldn't do it. Even though Baxter is my baby brother, he was the one with the bright ideas. So he decides we should form a human chain like circus performers and hoist up our point guard – Pipper, we called him – who was the smallest kid in our grade at the time. I still don't know to this day how we actually got Pipper up there, but, of course, that was the easy part. Getting him back down was another matter."

Mom giggled at that point, and Everett continued, adding a little more drama.

"Pipper retrieved our ball and threw it down, but then he kind of freaked out. He'd start running around on the roof, then he'd look over the edge, scream, and run around again. I guess he was suffering from vertigo! Baxter insisted I be the one to boot it home and get our dad, who in turn brought his extension ladder and a really bad temper."

Mom's giggle erupted into a tinkling laugh, and Dad chuckled. Even Holly was laughing.

Everett said, "Dad climbed up and tried coaxing Pipper

down the ladder for at least twenty minutes. Eventually, he had to admit defeat and call the fire department for a real rescue team. They brought Pipper down in the bucket of their snorkel truck and took him to the hospital for observation. Poor guy. He was a nervous wreck – didn't want to play with us for a good while after that – but we were just lucky he didn't fall off the roof and break his neck... And all that for a basketball!"

After some general hilarity, I heard Mom say, "You're staying for dinner then, Everett?" It was obvious that Mom loved him.

I couldn't help feel somewhat grateful to him myself. It seemed as if my family had forgotten about my misdemeanour, or at least taken a step toward forgiving it. No one mentioned it later, and even though I didn't join in the dinner conversation, I was spared accusing glances as long as Everett was there.

I just wished that my problem was as simple as a ball on a roof – that Dodie and I had really gone back to retrieve my forgotten basketball. While everyone dug into their stir-fry, I couldn't help but see Coach Nola's ghost raise her arm to take the foul shot.

CHAPTER FOURTEEN

Gossip must travel at the speed of light. Everyone in the entire school knew about my detentions by the next morning, even though detention hall was a windowless room where no one could look in to see who was serving. I started out trying to avoid a million and one questions, but by the end of the day, I was beginning to think it wasn't so bad being in trouble. People who basically ignored me on a regular basis were treating me like some kind of hero. They wanted to know if Mr. Portney had chased us with his mop as we were getting away and how loud Mr. Talbot had yelled. It seemed Dodie managed to avoid all of this by working in the science lab at lunch and asking to go to the library as soon as her class work was finished. When someone did ask her a question, she'd just stare at them and shake her head as if they weren't worthy of an answer. This pretty much left everyone turning to me for the details.

By three-thirty that afternoon, even I was growing tired of it – hero or not. I was ready to go home and shut my bedroom door firmly on the world, but there was still basketball practice to survive, and things were likely to get worse. I just didn't know how much worse.

It started in the change room when Dodie signalled that she needed to talk to me.

Karmyn caught the exchange and started in. "So, like what, are you two into romantic, moonlight extra practice or something?"

Dodie maintained her composure from earlier in the day,

bent down to lace her shoes and ignored the remark.

This noticeably irritated Karmyn, and before she could say anything else, I tried to deflect the heat away from Dodie. I swallowed hard and said, "What?"

Karmyn turned to me. "There's no way you forgot your ball, Summer. It's always the first thing you put in your bag after practice. So what were you two doing here after-hours?"

Roxx snorted as she pulled her jersey down over her sports bra. "Yeah, are you whistle kleptomaniacs or something? What else could you want in the gym office? Nothing there but ice packs and student records. Or were you trying to change Dodie's gym mark to an A?"

CJ and Faith laughed, and the twins exchanged glances.

Dodie stomped out of the change room, followed quickly by Val, but the rest of the girls waited to see what I was going to say. I shook my head, knowing it was the lamest thing I could do.

Karmyn hissed, "We told you, Summer, not to waste your time with her. You sneak in here to help her with her free throws and wind up with detentions. Serves you right."

It was obvious that Karmyn had made her own assumptions about why we'd been in the gym and it seemed safest to let her believe what she wanted, but I couldn't help being frustrated with her mean attitude.

I blurted out, "Why don't you just give her a break? What's Dodie ever done to you – or anyone?"

The minute I said it, I wanted to take it back. It was as if we were in some kind of movie where my empty revolver had just clicked and now Karmyn's gun was pointed at me. A sly little smile crossed her mouth.

Roxx was eager to jump in. "Dodie's a spaz and the most annoying person in the entire school. No one wants her around, and no one wants her on this team, except maybe you."

I forced myself to walk past them into the gym. It made no sense. Dodie was a target simply because she wasn't like them.

Admittedly, she hadn't been my favourite person either, but still...she was the one who agreed to come with me when I claimed I saw a ghost. How many other girls would do that and not accuse you of being nuts?

The minute I stepped into the gym, my eyes darted toward the bleachers. I relaxed a bit when they appeared to be empty. From the corner of my eye, I saw Dodie take an outside shot that missed the backboard totally, but the ball ricocheted in my direction.

Dodie chased after it, and when she was close enough, she whispered, "Summer, it may be scientifically possible that you really are seeing a ghost."

"What?" I said.

At that moment, the other girls came into the gym and Dodie dribbled off quickly in the opposite direction. My first urge was to follow her, but she glanced over her shoulder and shook her head at me. Coach Rogers blew his whistle, and although I tried to sidle over in Dodie's direction, she ignored me. I had to turn my attention to Coach Rogers' instructions for our first drill.

The practice turned out to be one enormous struggle. Between glancing at the bleachers too often, trying to catch Dodie's attention, and at the same time trying to avoid Karmyn, the drills seemed impossible to master. It wasn't until later, when we started our scrimmage and Dodie was once again relegated to the sidelines, that I became aware of something even more worrisome. The other players were acting as if I wasn't on the court at all. I knew I hadn't focused during the drills, but even when I was wide open calling for the ball, no one passed to me. The only basket I scored was on a rebound from one of Roxx's missed shots.

At one point, Coach Rogers smacked his forehead and yelled, "Summer, get in the play, will you? Or else go shoot foul shots over there with...uh...what's her...Dire Straits."

The very next play, I cut away from Karmyn, who was my

check, into the open key and called for the pass, but CJ ignored me and passed to Roxx again. At the end, I hung back out of the high-fives, even though our team was the winner of the scrimmage. I didn't understand what was happening.

Coach Rogers held me back when the other girls hit the change room. His reprimand was delivered in a macho tone. "I expect to see more effort next practice, Summer. The other girls are showing definite signs of improvement. I'm not seeing that from you." He looked at me for a minute, shoved his whistle in his mouth, chewed on it, then spat it out. "That's a surprise and a disappointment." He pointed at the change room, indicating he was finished talking to me.

By the time I started unlacing my shoes, Dodie was already barging out the change-room door. I wanted to call for her to wait, but I was fighting back tears from Coach Rogers' lecture. I couldn't let the other girls know that I was upset. I pretended that I had a knot in one of my laces and kept my head down, biting hard on my back teeth to prevent tears from spilling down my cheeks. *I will not cry, I will not cry*, I repeated to myself. A crimson heat flooded my face. No one spoke to me. The conversation swirled around me instead.

"That was a great practice." Karmyn beamed.

"Faith, you scored more baskets than anyone!" CJ pointed out.

"Yeah!" Roxx added. "Faith on fire!"

Everyone laughed.

Faith stopped reapplying eyeliner in the mirror, turned around and took a bow.

I raised my head and forced a smile. "Good job, Faith," I managed to say, but although Faith glanced at me as if she'd heard me over the laughter, she quickly turned back to the mirror.

Slinging her gym bag over her arm, Karmyn said to the group, "Things are a lot better when Dodie's not on the floor, eh?"

There was a slight hesitation before everyone, even Val, agreed.

I threw my shoes into my bag and headed out the door. I practically ran to the empty bleachers. I scanned them in both directions. I ran to the top of them and diagonally back down, making them bounce and creak under my weight. Nothing appeared. What had Dodie said to me, something about a scientific explanation for seeing Coach Nola's ghost? Breathing heavily, I waved my hands through the air as if maybe I could feel some kind of physical entity there, or better yet, actually summon Coach to appear and scare the daylights out of the rest of them. It would serve them right. Why did they have to be so mean?

I heard Karmyn's voice from the change room door. "She really is becoming just as weird as the Dodo-bird."

"Weird is too kind a word," I heard Roxx add.

And then in a voice I'm not certain I was meant to hear, Karmyn said, "Let's not pass to her next practice, either. I don't think we really need her after all."

I sat down hard on the bleachers. With all my might, I tried to remember what it had been like at the practice when Nola Blythe had said we would be provincial champs and she'd named me captain. It wasn't that long ago. It was there, right in the middle jump-ball circle of the gym. Why was there such emptiness around that memory now? As if it hadn't ever happened. As if my life before wasn't really my life. As if my old life was somewhere above me floating on the surface, and I was underwater, unable to emerge because of the tremendous weight of the water, unable to remember what *normal* felt like. All the water above me...a misery ocean... salt-water tears.

When Mr. Portney saw me sobbing on the bleachers, he called out, "Come on now, you better go on home." He didn't come close and he didn't say anything more, but he waited until he was sure I had picked up my bag and was on my way.

The next day at school, immediately following my detention, my homeroom teacher handed me a note that read: *Please report to Mrs. Chamber's office after morning announcements.* I had been booked to see the school guidance counsellor.

CHAPTER FIFTEEN

Mrs. Chamber was wearing a kind of silk kimono over top of her ankle-length denim skirt, and a pair of black lacquer chopsticks was stuck through the bun in her hair. When she caught me staring at the chopsticks, she pulled them out to allow me a closer look. They were decorated with delicate painted blossoms.

"I've recently started practising meditation," she said to me, "and it's really sparked my interest in the Eastern cultures. I find the meditation is an important part of de-stressing my day. Have you ever tried it, Summer?"

"No," I mumbled, and handed her back the chopsticks.

She stuck them back in her bun. "Thank you," she said with a fake relaxed smile. "Well, then." She cleared her throat. "Is there anything that is stressing you out right now? Anything you'd like to discuss? Sometimes, talking about your feelings can also be a very important tool in de-stressing. And none of us want to be stressed," she added and laughed.

If my mother had laughed that laugh, I would have classified it in the non-comfort zone – strained, nearly pained. It made me feel a little guilty, so I forced myself to make eye contact when I shrugged and said, "No, not really."

Mrs. Chamber nodded and continued. "We can talk about anything here. Maybe we should start with school. I looked over your last report card and your marks were very good; however, second term really sneaks up on some students. The reviewing from first term ends, and wham, a lot of new concepts get thrown at you. Are you struggling with any subjects right now?" She stopped and waited.

I could feel my eyebrows tense. I shook my head firmly. How was it that people could go on talking about things that seemed suddenly so meaningless to me and expect me to carry on a conversation with them? I saw a ghost. My teammates were ganging up on me because the only person I'd told about the ghost was someone they wanted to bully. How could I explain that to Mrs. Chamber? I crossed my arms over my chest.

Mrs. Chamber reached for a notepad that was on her desk and flipped through a couple of pages. Then she said, "I received a report that you were given some detentions this week and also that you were distraught last evening in the gym. Is there anything about either of those incidents that you'd like to share?"

She stopped as if she was waiting for me to catch up with her sudden switch of gears before she continued. "Mr. Talbot was concerned that he'd been a bit harsh with you, especially since this was your first time in any kind of trouble. You also have to understand that what you did was of a serious nature and it's his responsibility to ensure it won't happen again. I have to tell you that he was also concerned that you were found alone in the gym again last evening. Anything by way of explanation there?" she prompted, with a hint in her voice that confessing would be a good idea.

"I just like it in the gym," I mumbled. Was I supposed to tell her that I was invoking the spirit of my dead basketball coach?

"You'd rather be in the gym than, say, go home in the evening?" Mrs. Chamber was on a new tack. "Is there anything or anyone at home you're trying to avoid?"

I sighed, a bit exasperated. "Everything's fine at home."

She smiled. "That's excellent, then. Do you think it would be helpful if I contacted someone at your house about the school's concerns?"

My eyes shot up. "No!" I insisted.

"Is there any particular reason you're feeling that way?" Mrs. Chamber asked, her own eyes focused sharply on mine.

"There's nothing wrong. It would just make my parents, who are already upset about my detentions, even more upset."

"I see," Mrs. Chamber said and reached for another notepad on her desk, on which she jotted something. "Then you can trust our conversation will be just between us." She smiled brightly and raised an eyebrow as if to say that now we could get serious about the matter at hand.

I licked my lips and stared at my hands.

"So, Summer, you really love basketball?"

"Yes."

"Perhaps you're still grieving about Ms. Blythe's accident."

I took in a sharp breath.

"I see," said Mrs. Chamber. She put her notebook back on her desk and reached for her box of tissues. "It's very important to complete the grieving cycle before we can be whole again." She tilted the tissues in my direction. "If you need these, please feel free to use them."

For some reason, her gesture made me really angry. She had no idea what was going on, but she was acting as if she'd solved the "Summer conundrum." She would report back to Principal Talbot that my problems could be summarized in a single word. Grief.

Mrs. Chamber must have noticed my anger, because she immediately said, "I can arrange for a proper grief counsellor, Summer. Someone who deals with this kind of matter every day."

"No, I'm fine, thank you," I said. "Just because you miss someone doesn't mean you have to dial up a grief counsellor, does it?"

Mrs. Chamber's mouth opened to answer, but then she closed it, along with her eyes. She took a deep, deep breath and let it out slowly. When she opened her eyes again, she shook her head in response to my question and immediately said, "Well then, Summer, I'm going to ask that you check in with me periodically, and if there's anything you ever want to talk about, my door is always open. Well, not literally, but figuratively speaking, of course. I do go home at night." She laughed at her own little joke and then turned suddenly serious. "Also, you should know that Coach Rogers is being informed that he must be the last one to leave the premises after practice. Because he's not on staff here, I guess he didn't realize that it is his responsibility to ensure everyone is safely out of the building before leaving himself. Just a little heads-up there. You are to leave the building immediately after practice in the future."

For a split second I wondered if the whole session had been conducted just to tell me that. *Mr. Portney does not want to have to clean around girls crying on the bleachers.* I must have outwardly smiled at my interior joke, because Mrs. Chamber made one last attempt.

"Anything you'd care to share before you go back to class, Summer?"

I forced my face into neutral and shook my head. Before I'd closed the door behind me, Mrs. Chamber was furiously scribbling on her notepad. I had the urge to flee the school as I walked down the hallway to my locker. What would be the punishment for skipping out on top of everything else? I really didn't care at all. Let them call my parents. Let them all wonder where I was. Maybe I could just go down by the riverbank, build a snow fort and stay there all night. Then they'd be sorry. The school would be responsible. I could freeze to death out there. Then Karmyn and her comrades could feel bad for the rest of their lives! I slammed my locker door shut, and there was Dodie. She jumped from the loud metal bang.

"Yikes, Mrs. Chamber give you a hard time?" she said sympathetically.

I felt tears welling up again. Why was I becoming so emotional? I forced myself to shrug it off. I looked at Dodie, and she seemed oddly dishevelled, like she'd come to school without combing her hair. She was wearing an old sweatshirt

I'd never seen before.

Dodie said, "Let's sneak into the back carrels in the library. I have to talk to you."

I scanned the hall. It was empty. "Dodie, what are you doing out of class? You're going to get into trouble because of me."

She waved her hand in the air as if she was swatting mosquitoes. "I finished all my math. Powlesland thinks I'm in the art room doing work for the Learning Fair. Don't sweat it."

"Dodie! You're going to get *me* into more trouble then." My thoughts of running away and hiding had dissipated.

"You're already in trouble, Summer. You're seeing ghosts!"

"Okay," I sighed. "But I haven't seen her since. I don't think I'm going to ever again."

"You might be right, but you might not be," Dodie said, adjusting her glasses.

"Thanks," I muttered.

"I've been researching non-stop since the other night."

"What do you mean?"

"Internet, library books, even went to the university library last evening – trying to find out what I could about ghosts. My dad drove me. He thought I was working on a school project."

Dodie and I checked to make sure the librarian was working in her office, and then we snuck into a back carrel, out of earshot.

When we were settled, Dodie whispered, "It's possible that ghost appearances can be explained scientifically, Summer, so I believe that you are seeing a ghost. But it's not like Coach has come out of her grave. Sorry," she added when she saw the look on my face.

"Scientists are using these really sensitive machines at 'haunted sites' and they're measuring magnetic fields and stuff. There are real measurable disturbances. They talk about place memory, where the actual environment holds the memory of something, kind of like taking a photograph – an image gets left behind because there's energy left behind. Especially if someone dies in an extreme way…you know…the way Coach Nola did," she added softly. "The only thing that's still not clear to me is why she's here and not where the accident happened. How could that energy be projecting back to Garvin?"

I shivered and clutched my elbows. This scientific explanation was giving me the creeps. Maybe somewhere in the back of my brain I was still hoping I hadn't really seen her – that it had been a trick of the dim light and my imagination. Again, I was forced to try to figure out why she'd appeared to me. And me only. I asked Dodie if she had an answer.

She took a deep breath and excitedly plunged into her next theory. "Well, it could be that some people are just more perceptive, Summer. You know, maybe mediums and psychics and whatnot aren't just a big hoax." Dodie's voice was rising above a whisper.

I put my finger to my lips and shushed her.

She lowered her voice. "It could also be that out of all of us, you're the one that cared the most about Coach. There is the theory that the emotional charge projected at the time of someone's death can be received telepathically by someone far away. There are lots of stories about someone dying at war overseas and their loved one seeing them at that moment." Dodie squinted as if her brain was working overtime. "But once again," she added, "that doesn't quite fit our situation because Coach is appearing after the fact."

I covered my ears. "Stop, Dodie! I don't think I want to hear anything more about this," I hissed.

Dodie sighed and nodded. "I understand, Summer. It must feel very strange. But from all my research, I've come to one conclusion: I don't think you should be afraid. I don't believe the ghost means any harm. Okay?"

I took a deep breath and nodded. We managed to sneak back out of the library without being caught. Maybe my luck was changing.

CHAPTER SIXTEEN

Coach Rogers booked our first exhibition scrimmage game less than a week later. Despite all that had been going wrong, I was very excited. The sun was shining brightly that day, and the snow was melting off the school roof. Water dripping in the middle of January in Manitoba was enough to lift anyone's spirits, but I had the extra bonus of anticipating the after-school game. Every time I thought about it during class that day, my stomach felt as agitated as Monday's wash-load. It wasn't long, however, before I found myself hung out to dry.

Coach Rogers chewed on his whistle and wrote things on his clipboard as we ran our warm-up drill that evening. He had rap music pumping from the gymnasium sound system, which Karmyn said was her idea. The heavy beat added to the adrenalin in our bodies and drowned out the sound of bouncing balls and squeaking shoes on the hardwood floor. The opposition from nearby Stoneville had a warm-up huddle cheer that was swallowed by the booming bass.

The music switched off as the two-minute warning buzzer sounded and we headed to our bench. My heart flip-flopped with excitement. We stripped off our warm-up shirts, tucked in our jerseys, gulped a few mouthfuls of water, and then Coach Rogers made circles in the air with his clipboard to gather us in a semi-circle around him.

"I based starting lineup on what I saw at the last practice," he stated. "So it's Karmyn at point guard. Roxx and CJ, you're wings. Roxx, take the right side." He looked up from his clipboard, and his eyes met mine but then moved on to settle on the twins. "Trish, right?" he said to one. Tracy pointed at her sister. Coach Rogers looked at the other. "Trish and Faith, I want you in post. Faith, right side, and you take the jump ball as well. Okay, girls, stay on your checks and let's do this! One, two, three…"

"Invaders!" everyone shouted. The word stuck in my throat. I wasn't starting the game! I'd always taken first jump ball in the past, if for no other reason than that I was the tallest on the team. My butt thudded onto the bench. I snuck a glance to where my parents were seated on the bleachers. They were both looking at me, their heads cocked to one side, so I quickly focused on retying my already-tied shoes.

Next to me, Dodie whispered, "Why aren't you starting, Summer?"

I shrugged and tugged at my socks.

"He's nuts," Dodie whispered. "Totally."

Not knowing how to respond, I said nothing and sat hunched over so my parents wouldn't be able to catch my eye.

We were down 10–4 before Coach Rogers made his first substitution. Then he subbed all of us from the bench, Dodie, Val, Tracy and me, leaving Trish on the floor in post. All the strong players on the first line came off and Dodie, who hadn't been allowed to play at any of Coach Rogers' practices, was told to be point guard and dribble the ball up the court. Every time she crossed the centre line, the ball was either stolen right out of her hands, intercepted on the pass, or was turned over because she simply lost control of the ball while dribbling, and Stoneville pounced on it. Almost every time the opposition took control of the ball, they beat our haphazard defence and scored. Val was intimidated and hung back off her check. Trish was too tired to be effective. Tracy chose that shift to show concern for Trish's well-being. Dodie continued to try her best but was called for numerous fouls as she swiped at the ball in her frustration. I couldn't defend against three or more players;

someone on the opposing team was always open to score. Five minutes of play went by before I managed to touch the ball on a defensive rebound. I passed to Dodie, but she lost it again as soon as she dribbled over the centre line. That was the only time I had the ball in my hands on the entire shift.

The worst part of the humiliation was that Dodie's mother, who sat at the opposite end of the bleachers to my parents, shouted out an endless supply of irritating comments in an otherwise quiet gym. "Keep your head up, Dodie! Pass the ball quicker! Run! Run! Help her out, girls! Get in the game! Watch out for number four. Behind you! Behind you! Arms up! Don't let her take the ball away like that! Protect the ball! Shoot the ball!" She must have been more exhausted than any of us.

Coach Rogers paced back and forth in front of the bench and smacked his forehead a lot. Karmyn and the others didn't seem to be paying the slightest attention to our struggles on the court. The score was 24–4 before Coach subbed us off. He told Trish to stay on for a third shift, and then he bent down in front of the bench and told us we'd just played the worst basketball he'd ever witnessed in his entire coaching career.

For the first time since the basketball season began, Dodie hung her head down and could not look up at Coach Rogers. After he'd turned his focus back to the court, I patted Dodie's shoulder.

She didn't raise her head, she just muttered, "Yes, in his entire brilliant coaching *career*, he's never seen the likes of us! Back when he was coaching – who was it that he coached, Shaq or Michael Jordan? No! Wait! I think it was the varsity boys at our local high school! Back then, he never saw the likes of us."

Despite my discouragement and fatigue, I smirked in response. At least he hadn't destroyed Dodie's sense of humour.

"Like you said, he's nuts!" I whispered. "Loco, demented, cuckoo. Crazier than me, even."

Dodie didn't laugh. She didn't even smile.

We didn't get to play any more in the first half. The score at half-time was 35–10. In our huddle, Coach Rogers told us that the first line out was to try the give-and-go play over and over since Karmyn seemed to be the only one who could score. Then he said, "Second shift, I want you to try and get the ball across the centre line and then pass into the post positions instead." He turned to me and said, "Supposedly your last coach referred to you as a secret weapon, Summer. You can stop keeping the secret any time now. Get your head in the game."

Karmyn and Roxx covered their hands with their mouths, but their shoulders shook with laughter. I could feel the red flush spreading from my neck upwards. A fuming surge coursed through me. How was I supposed to get my head in the game when we couldn't even move the ball into an offensive position? Dodie hadn't even been allowed to play at practice. How could anyone expect her to play now? All the strong players were on the other line and they weren't exactly doing so well themselves with only five baskets in the half. As the other girls headed onto the court to start the second half, I turned back to our bench and kicked my water bottle. It whacked a bench leg and went spinning in a circle away from the bench. I left it there and sat down.

Coach Rogers yelled, "Whose water bottle is that? Get it off the court!"

Dodie jumped to retrieve it and tucked it behind my feet.

"Thanks," I muttered.

"I wish Coach Nola would come," she said in a fierce whisper. "She could scare the heck out of him."

The image of Nola Blyth's ghost surfaced in my head like a tidal wave. I trembled. What if her ghost was actually here and witnessing my huge sucking failure? I covered my face with my hands and rubbed hard at my eyes, trying to erase what I saw in my brain. It wouldn't go away.

"Summer!" Coach Rogers was yelling at me. "You're on!"

At least ten minutes had passed in the half without my noticing. I glanced at the scoreboard: 47–15. Who had scored baskets? I didn't even know. I ran onto the court. I looked down the stretch of bleachers. There was no ghost, but suddenly everything seemed in sharper focus. The orange uniforms of the opposing team shimmered as if they were a fire I had to put out. The ball seemed alive. I gritted my teeth. Stoneville had possession. I intercepted their first pass and power dribbled down for a layup. I missed it, but grabbed my own rebound and sank it. My teammates all swarmed me with high fives, but by that time the opposition had already done a quick break and came scoring back on us. Coach Rogers yelled from the bench, but I didn't hear what he said. I just knew I had to get the ball and score.

I ran to Dodie as she started to dribble out of our defensive end and said, "Pass me the ball before we get to half-court, okay?"

Dodie nodded.

I ran ahead and she passed it to me before the other team could press her. I wasn't going to allow the turn-overs any more. I drove in to the hoop, shot and was fouled.

Standing at the line, I glanced over at my parents who were nodding and Dad gave me the thumbs-up. Dodie's mother yelled, "You can do this, Summer! Focus. Take your time."

Two swishes. I'd scored four points in less than a minute. After that, I poured on every ounce of energy I had, covering the entire key defensively. Offensively, I carried the ball and never passed off. Sometimes the opposition stopped me, but often they didn't. I scored another four baskets before my shift was over. That was more points than we'd scored in the first half. 51–27. We were winning the half. Coach Rogers left me on the court when it came time for subs. I played the rest of the second half, and, although Karmyn never passed me the ball once, I still managed to make four more baskets on rebounds and passes from other players. Final score 51–38. Not a bad finish for something that had started out so dismally.

At the end of the game, Coach Rogers nodded his head at me and said, "I could see some potential out there, *Withering Heights*."

As we lined up to shake hands, Karmyn cut in front of me and said over her shoulder, "You figured out you have to ditch the Dodo-bird, eh? She is the most unbelievable loser in the history of the sport."

Karmyn sounded just like her step-dad-to-be, complete with his habit of offensive nick-naming. I felt a pang of guilt thinking about the second half of the game and how I never passed the ball or let Dodie try to cross half with it. The guilt lasted only a few seconds, as the ref announced me as the player of the game for our team. The ref shook my hand and gave me a coupon for free pizza. My parents stepped in and took a photograph. I had done what I had to do. It was best for the team that I scored those baskets.

Everyone congratulated me. Even Karmyn grudgingly said, "Way to go."

Dodie edged her way toward me and smiled. "You did great, Summer."

"Thanks, Dodie," I said. "Uh, so did you," I added, but my tone of voice sounded about as sincere as one of my mother's forced laughs. The thought crossed my mind to invite Dodie to share my free pizza, but I glanced over at Karmyn and Roxx and they were watching me, so I just smiled and turned away from her. Fortunately, my parents were standing there vibrating with pride when I turned away, so I didn't appear too rude. Mom gushed that she was so proud of me and Dad gave me a bear hug. With my nose squished into his shoulder, I noticed the numbers on the scoreboard start to flash erratically. Our final score Guests 51, Home 38 flashed off and on several times, and then the numbers started changing so quickly you could barely read them. It stopped at 51–38 for a few brief flashes and then started randomly changing again. I looked to the scorekeeper's table, but there was no one sitting at the control panel. The scoreboard seemed to have a mind of its own. I was about to point it out to my dad. That's when I saw her.

She was sitting on the bleachers again! She wasn't looking at the scoreboard, though. She was staring right at me or right through me with the same sad, lifeless expression, as if the weight of the afterworld was on her shoulders.

I pulled away from my dad and gulped for air. I covered my eyes.

Mom murmured, "I guess we're embarrassing her, Paul." Then she took a closer look at me and said, "Summer, are you okay?"

My head was swimming. The coconut smell drifted in a thin wavery waft past my nostrils. I pinched my nose. The smell wasn't unpleasant, it just didn't seem of this earth, and for some reason, it was frightening to breathe it in. Coach Nola's ghost stood and made as if she was going to shoot at the basket behind me from way across the court. She was lining up the shot. I turned my head to see the basket behind me, half expecting to glimpse a ghostly whiteness pass through the hoop. I licked my lips. My tongue rasped dryly over them, salt-laden.

"Thirsty," I breathed out.

"Paul, grab her water bottle for her. You look exhausted. Summer? Are you okay?" Mom repeated. "Maybe you overexerted yourself."

I looked for Dodie, but she was gone. I pointed in the direction of where Coach's ghost was standing.

Dad handed me the water bottle and glanced to where I indicated. The scoreboard was flashing the final score again. Dad said, "It's not bad for your first game this year, Summer. You'll improve on that as you go along. You looked great out there, especially in the second half."

He couldn't see Coach Nola either.

I closed my eyes and drained the dregs of my water bottle. When I opened them, she was coming steadily toward me – a look of absolute pathos on her face. I held my breath. Then she simply disappeared into a wisp of nothingness. I blinked hard and felt my teeth start to chatter. The gymnasium was emptying out. No one had seen her except me.

"Where is your sweatshirt, Summer?" I could hear Mom fussing around me, unzipping my gym bag and rummaging through it, but it seemed like she and Dad were off in another world.

I had been so certain I'd seen Coach Nola for the last time. Why had she come back? And why was she still so changed? I knew that if my life was cut short, I would be sad, too. But if she was sad because her life was over, why wouldn't she want everyone to see her? Why was I the only one who was invited to witness her terrible woe?

CHAPTER SEVENTEEN

That evening, I could barely eat my dinner. Mom reached over and felt my forehead at least a half-dozen times. Each time she did, Dad would put down his *Electronics Today* magazine and say something like "She's fine, Olivia. That was her first game of the season. She's just tired. Right, kiddo?"

Each time, I nodded my head in response but said nothing.

Mom finally conceded and went upstairs to change. When she came down, she said, "Okay, Dad and I have a meeting this evening, and then I'm going straight to work. I want you to get right into bed if you have no homework, understood? No TV, no Internet. I know you're just coming off your grounding. This is not more grounding. I just want you to get some rest." Then she called upstairs, "Holly, are you home for the evening?"

"Yes, Mom!" Holly called down.

"Good. Summer needs to go straight to bed tonight. Okay? So keep your stereo low."

"Yes, Mom!" Holly repeated.

As soon as Mom and Dad were out the door, Holly cranked her music. I tried to lie down on my bed and close my eyes, but the ghostly image of Coach Nola seemed to be pasted to the back of my eyelids. I stood and paced my room. Over the moon – that's how I should have been feeling. I'd been named player of the game! I grabbed my gym bag, found the free pizza coupon and set it on my desk next to my team photo. No relief – nothing but unease churning in my guts and an itchy twitching in my brain. I turned to the window. Almost every yard across the street had sprung a snowman, a result of the unseasonably warm day. I unlatched my window and cranked it open. The air had a moist, almost tropical feel to it, despite it being the dead middle of winter. The wind gusted from the south and I could still sense the remnants of the sun that had shone earlier that day. I breathed deeply, but it wasn't enough to settle my stomach or scratch my itching brain.

I went downstairs, slipped my parka and boots over top of my pyjamas. Outside the front door, I started to roll a small ball for a snowman body. I suddenly stopped. If I built a snowman, Mom would know I hadn't gone straight to bed. I carried the snowball to the backyard fence and dumped it into the neighbour's yard. I could see Holly through her bedroom window, studying at her desk. The faint beat of her music could be heard from where I stood below. She wasn't even aware I was out of the house. A sudden urge to run overtook me. A senseless urge – I was trying to run away from a ghost. No one can outrun a ghost. I sprinted out of the yard and careened through slushy, half-frozen ruts down our street and onto the next before I knew what I was doing. In five minutes, I'd arrived at Dodie's. I panted outside her house for another five minutes, not knowing how to proceed. I didn't want to ring her doorbell for fear that her mother had found out about our last escapade in the gym with the custodian. At that moment, I resented Dad for not letting me have my own cell phone, but then I doubted Dodie had one either. I'd never been past the entrance of her house, but I knew she was an only child, so I went around to the back and saw frilly pink curtains on one of the bedroom windows. I packed some snow and threw it lightly against her window. The splat dripped down the glass pane. A second later, Dodie's face appeared. She was cupping her hands around her eyes to see into the darkened backyard.

I felt a rush of relief to see her framed there. Waving frantically, I sprang forward. She slid her window open and leaned down to speak through the small opening.

"Now what, Summer?" she whispered loudly. The tone of her voice was not unwelcoming even though she skipped the niceties.

I knelt down in the snow under her window and realized I was still wearing my pyjama pants. My knees were instantly soaked and cold.

I said, "Dodie, I saw her again. Tonight. At the end of the game. I thought it was over. That she was gone. But she was there, the same as ever. Only this time she started walking, well, more like floating, toward me. Then just disappeared."

Dodie did not interrupt while I blurted this out. "Dodie," I finally said, "what if she never goes away?"

"Hang on, Summer. I'm coming."

A few moments later, Dodie came out in her coat and boots. She said, "I told my dad I'm going to the corner store. Come on, I'll have to buy a chocolate bar for him, or he'll tell my mom I went out. She's at work, and I'm supposed to be pasting hearts on her Volunteer Tea posters for the hospital auxiliary." She paused. "Are you getting frightened, Summer? You know, it can't hurt you. According to my research, ghosts leave minimal energy traces. The guys who go around with all that ghost-detecting equipment acknowledge thumps or scratching or maybe a book pushed off a shelf, but in theory, that's about all the physical effect a ghost can have. It can't channel enough energy to hurt a human."

Dodie slid her glasses up her nose and took a hard look at me.

I responded, "I don't think I'm really scared she's going to hurt me. I'm just scared that she exists. Because I don't know why she exists and it is very scary being the only one who sees her. That just makes me think I'm losing my mind, no matter what the theories say."

We trudged down the street. I turned and checked behind me a couple of times.

Dodie grabbed my arm and dragged me forward. "Apart from the staircase, it has only appeared in the gym? Not in your house?" Dodie questioned, sounding like a detective.

I nodded.

"So, if we were to hold another séance, the attic would likely be the best place. We'd never pull it off in the gym with Mr. Portney lurking there."

I tugged back on Dodie's arm and forced her to stop. "Dodie! You were the one who was set against the first séance. You said we didn't know what we were messing with. You were right!"

"Yeah, well, it's too late for not messing with it, Summer! Maybe messing with it again is the only way we can discover why it's here."

"But the other girls freaked, remember?"

We had reached the corner store, and I shivered. The south wind no longer felt balmy, just damp and bone-chilling. "You go in, Dodie. I'm wearing my pyjamas."

"So you are!" Dodie exclaimed. "I hadn't even noticed."

Dodie came out with a bag full of chocolate bars and held it open for me to choose one. I picked a Bounty bar and the moment I peeled back the wrapper, I flung the whole thing into the snow.

"Summer, why'd you do that?" Dodie cried.

"Uh…I…don't know. I…that's the smell! Every time she comes, I smell coconut."

"Whoa, that's totally weird!" Dodie picked the bar out of the snow. "Mind if I eat the part that's still in the wrapper? I love these."

"Dodie, *that's* totally weird!"

"I know," she said and shoved half the bar in her mouth. Then she laughed and almost choked.

I laughed too and realized I hadn't laughed in what seemed like forever.

My laughter made Dodie laugh even harder, and suddenly the two of us were hysterically falling in the snow and fighting over the bag of chocolate bars. Finally we stopped and took deep breaths.

As soon as Dodie could speak again, she said, "Okay, about this coconut smell..."

At that, I started to laugh and cry at the same time. I was colder than ever. My pyjamas were soaked and clung to my legs as we started back toward Dodie's house. Every few meters, I had to wipe the tears from my eyes. As I tried to describe the wafting coconut smell, I sounded crazy even to myself.

"Have a bar with caramel in it, then," Dodie said and opened the bag. "Look, Summer, let's drop all the scientific reasoning – which is very hard for me to do, but part of science is being able to remove the blinders and open your eyes to possibility. We'd still believe in a geocentric universe if not for open-minded scientists like Copernicus, right?"

"I suppose so," I managed to say as the caramel stuck to my teeth. Dodie's mind sure bounced about; just who was Copernicus?

"So for a theory's sake," she continued, "let's assume it's not an energy trace but a human spirit. Maybe it's just coming to watch you play. I mean, you did really well in the game tonight." Dodie's voice trailed off, and a furrow formed in the space between her eyebrows.

I didn't know how to interpret her frown, but I couldn't help but feel a pang of guilt. "Well, she would be coming to watch the whole team," I corrected.

"Yes, but then you'd think the whole team could see it. Let's also assume that it's capable of revealing itself to whomever it pleases. And it pleases to reveal itself to you."

I wanted to ask Dodie if Coach Nola was really there to see me play, and if I'd had such a great game, then why was she so sad? But I didn't have the heart to say anything further after not letting Dodie do her job as point guard and carry the ball up the court. Instead, I changed the subject lamely. "If that's the case, Dodie, if she's a spirit with functioning thoughts, then you'll have to stop calling her *it* and call her *she*."

"Okay," Dodie responded. "She. Coach Nola," she said and

looked at me meaningfully.

"You believe me, don't you Dodie?"

She shrugged and nodded. "*Our doubts are traitors.*"

"What?"

"Shakespeare," she replied and sighed.

"Dodie, what are you talking about?"

"While researching, I read some Shakespeare – there are several ghosts in his work. His apparitions are the spirits of the deceased with messages for the living. Not very scientific, but, of course, Shakespeare was a playwright. Why would he write in a ghost unless it had details to deliver? Shakespeare was also a genius, so maybe he had the inside track on ghosts and their purpose."

I sighed. "So now you think she has a message for me?"

"It's a theory."

"Dodie, you're making my head spin."

"Summer, no one's head is spinning faster than yours. That's a given."

I laughed again. I couldn't help myself. Dodie somehow made it all seem manageable. It struck me in that moment, that Dodie was the most fearless kid I'd ever known. And to think that everyone, including me, had pegged her for a wimp.

The next moment, it entered my head that the reason Coach Nola's spirit had appeared so sad at the end of the game was because we'd lost. She'd made the scoreboard go weird, hadn't she? During the séance, hadn't Roxx asked her how we could win the Provincials? How could we win Provincials if we couldn't win an exhibition game? Was Coach Nola trying to communicate how? Was that her message? Perhaps it was because she'd named me captain that I was the only one who could see her. It was my job to receive and deliver her message. But so far she hadn't talked. How was I supposed to understand? Was it my job to interpret what her message would be if she could talk? Until I could do that, maybe she wouldn't be able to rest.

I sighed so hard it was almost a hiccup.

Dodie gave me a strange look.

I stood in the damp wind, shivering in my wet pyjama pants, and said, "Okay, Dodie, other than holding another séance, how can we figure out her message for certain? No assumptions. No theories. Just certainty."

"I'm working on that part, Summer. I'm working on it."

CHAPTER EIGHTEEN

"Summer Widden, what in the world?" Mom stood over me at the breakfast table, holding my soaking wet pyjama pants in one hand with a laundry basket perched on her other hip. She'd just come off nights and should have been sleeping in bed. After I'd left Dodie the night before, I had been so frazzled, I'd stripped off the wet PJs and left them in a soggy ball on the floor in the corner of my bedroom.

I stammered, "I…uh…"

Mom's lips were pursed into a tight little *O*, and there wasn't a tinkle of laughter anywhere in her vicinity.

If Dodie were here, she'd have reeled off some kind of cover story by now. I made my attempt. "You know how I felt so hot after the game last evening? Well, for some strange reason, it got even worse later. Waves of heat. Maybe I had a temp. I just went out the back door to cool off, but I slipped because I guess the roof had been dripping yesterday in the warmth, and then the water froze, and anyway, I landed in the wet snow."

The words sounded so lame coming out of my mouth that I thought for sure I was headed for another grounding. Instead, Mom put down the laundry basket to place her palm on my forehead again. She seemed satisfied but added, "Call me from school this morning if you're not feeling well."

I nodded and pretended to read the back of the cereal box as she headed to the laundry room.

When she returned, she said, "I just remembered you have

the season opener tonight, right?"

I was shocked that I'd forgotten about the game that morning, but my mind had hamster-wheeled around for hours during the night, long after I should have been asleep. By morning my thoughts drifted, unfocused and sleep-deprived.

Mom continued, "I'm not sure you should play, Summer."

"I'm fine this morning, Mom! I have to play! They can't win without me." I sat straight and tried to look lively. I wished Dad hadn't already left for work. I needed an ally. "I can't miss the game. Coach Rogers will kill me if I'm not there. He'll cut me, Mom."

"I don't imagine he'll cut you for being ill," she reasoned, with a hint of sarcasm. "And if – as you so modestly claim – they can't win without you, how could he possibly cut you?"

Before I continued to plead with her, I had the good sense to blush, even though my mother didn't understand what might truly be at stake. "Please, Mom! You're the one who hoped this basketball thing wasn't another fleeting fad!"

She sniffed and busied herself at the kitchen counter. She didn't like me quoting her to support my argument. I held my breath. Maybe I was learning some Dodie tactics after all.

She sighed and said, "Well, see how your day goes…"

"I'll be fine!" I assured her, exhaling.

I was more than fine when I saw Holly and Everett arrive in the Spartans gym for the pre-game warm-up. Holly waved with two hands from the bleachers and Everett saluted me with a swish sign. Dad and Mom were also there giving me the thumbs-up. My confidence swelled and quelled some of the butterflies in my stomach. I couldn't tell if I was nervous about the game or about the ghost. Maybe Holly and Everett would witness her ghostly appearance; better yet, maybe they could somehow obstruct it. Standing back on the court again,

I realized how much of a distraction waiting for a ghost to appear can be to your game. I wanted to know if Coach Nola really had a message, but more than that, I wanted her to not have one and just go peacefully away.

Dodie rushed over to me and said, "You have a whole cheering section." Then she added just loud enough for me to hear, "A flesh and blood one. Not a ghoul amongst them. Especially *not* your sister's boyfriend!"

"I didn't think you paid much attention to boys," I said quietly, but in mock surprise.

"Only if they're perfect scientific examples of Darwin's theory of natural selection," she responded. "Or, to be more specific...if they're really hot!"

Fearless Dodie rides again! I waited for her to blush, but she didn't. I high-fived her, but as I turned around I caught sight of Karmyn and Roxx, smirks on their faces, whispering and staring at us. Karmyn rolled her eyes at me. I couldn't risk not getting passes from her today. As I attempted to dribble away from Dodie, I pumped my ball so hard into the hardwood floor, it sprang above my shoulders and I had to fight to gain control of it again before I could complete my layup. Dodie didn't seem to pay any attention to them at all. A moment later, Karmyn's ball *accidentally* connected with the back of Dodie's head.

"Oh, sorry," she said and managed to keep a straight face while Roxx snickered behind her.

Why did they have to be so cruel? How could I be expected to watch my back on two fronts? The paranormal and the abnormal? Why didn't the apparition haunt them for a while to see if their capacity for bullying could be limited if they were scared out of their wits?

I was so frustrated and angry I committed two personal fouls against the opposing Spartans in the first three minutes of the game. Coach Rogers benched me for the next ten. Dodie sat beside me.

"Any sign of *her*?" she asked.

I shook my head. If the score had anything to do with Coach Nola's appearances, she should have been blasting up and down the court in a vaporous frenzy. We were down by twenty points and not even able to keep the ball in our offensive end long enough to take a shot. Karmyn was stomping her foot and giving Coach Rogers evil glares as if our team's sucking was totally his fault. CJ and Faith seemed to be defeated already, putting in a half-effort. Val was holding her side like she had a stitch in it.

"*Withering Heights*," he finally said, "get ready to sub in there for the round wounded one."

As I squatted at the scorekeeper's table, I saw Holly clapping in the stands. "Yay, Summer!" she cheered. Everett made a power fist and rotated it a couple of times above his head.

"I've got number seven," the tallest Spartan yelled, already crouched in triple threat position, pointing at me as I walked onto the court. *Walk on as a winner*, I reminded myself, Coach Nola's words, not mine. Straightening my shoulders, I gave my teammates high-fives and felt a little ripple of energy run through us.

We battled it out. I scored five unanswered in a row in the second half, but we were still eight points down with two minutes left to play. Coach Rogers smacked his head and called a time out when Faith's shot was blocked and deflected out of bounds. "Okay, girls, I know you're tired. Some of you have played practically the whole game."

I glanced at the bench and realized Dodie hadn't played at all. Panting and wiping the sweat off my face, I reasoned that she wouldn't have been able to keep pace out there, so perhaps it was for the best. She handed me my water bottle and smiled almost apologetically. I couldn't let myself feel sorry for her.

Coach Rogers was talking, getting more intense with each sentence. "We can press at this stage of the game, so that's what we're going to do. It's the only way we'll pull out the win. We're giving the ball to Summer on this inbound under the basket. She's going to score, and as soon as they have control, you're on your man, and you're not letting that ball over half-court. Got it? The second they pass that ball in, you're all over it. Got it? Don't pussyfoot around like a bunch of old ladies. You don't quit until we steal and score again and again. Got it?"

He was practically shaking us by the shoulders with the loud intensity of his voice. Parents from both sides of the bleachers were glancing over, and the opposition parents were shaking their heads in disbelief. I didn't care. I strode onto the court determined to turn this game around. The first play was all mine. He'd told the team to give the ball to me!

I cut into position under the basket, and Roxx was about to pass the ball to me when Karmyn cut in too. Roxx passed her the ball. Karmyn laid it up, but the ball circled the rim and popped out. I grabbed the rebound and shot it in. Two points! There was only a split second before we had to press. I yelled at both Roxx and Karmyn, "Coach said the play was to me!" Furious, I intercepted the very next pass and sank another two-pointer. The opposition started to panic. Four points separated us. Just over a minute to play. Their coach was yelling instructions about how to break the press. It failed when I took the ball right out of their point guard's hands and shot from outside the key and sank it. Time out from the opposition. We ran to our bench. Holly and Everett were on their feet, clapping.

Coach Rogers gave me a high-five and said, "That's it, Summer. The rest of you, pick it up! They're going to try the split-off on the throw-in. Get position on them by stepping partly in front of them as soon as you can and intercept. Summer, you're under the hoop on possession! Pressure them, and don't let them cross half!"

We put our fists in a circle and yelled, "Invaders!" It was the first time we'd done anything resembling a determined team cheer since Coach Nola's death. With my adrenalin pumping,

I couldn't believe that I'd ever seen her ghost. It was all a trick of the light, or maybe it was just me waiting to really play basketball again and imagining her in my head.

Faith lunged at the pass and got the ball. I headed for the hoop but had to come back when the Spartans swarmed her in desperation. Somehow, she bounce-passed it to me under their legs. One of the swarmers split off and fouled me from behind as I attempted to sink it from the top of the key. The whistle blew. Shooting two. Ten seconds on the clock.

I was panting so hard there were little spots in front of my eyes. I had to sink both foul shots to tie. I bent over and rested with my hands on my knees while both teams lined up. Focus. The first shot wobbled on the rim and went in. The crowd let out an audible gasp. The sound seemed to roar in my ears like crashing ocean waves.

"Shooting one, play off the rim," the ref said as he tossed me the ball for my second shot.

I was going to tie this game and be the come-back queen! Focus.

From the bench, Dodie yelled, "You can do this, Summer!"

Her voice ripped through the hush that had fallen over the stands and made my shoulders shudder. I blasted a look back at the bench that indicated she should be quiet. Coach Rogers berated her for breaking my concentration.

I smelled coconut.

From the corner of my eye, the scoreboard dimmed, pulsed, dimmed, pulsed. *She* was there under the hoop. I stared at her and blinked hard, willing her to disappear. I gulped for air, put my head down and saw each little dimple in the ball. My hands trembled and the dimples blurred. The ref started to count seconds off with his arm, waiting for me to shoot. I put the ball up. It went in. I met Nola Blythe's eyes, and they were pathetically void of exaltation.

"No shot! No shot!" the ref yelled and jumped into the key for the ball. "Green violates." He was pointing at my feet.

I'd gone way over the foul line, as if I'd fallen into the shot – or been drawn in by some ghostly magnet. I hadn't even noticed. I could have sworn I hadn't moved. The Spartans had possession, still ten seconds on the clock. My legs refused to engage. The Spartans rushed past me, and the buzzer sounded to end the game. A one-point loss. Coach Nola was dissipating like mist in a breeze.

CHAPTER NINETEEN

In the change room after the game, the twins stood on either side of me and patted my shoulders. I should have been more downcast about losing the game by one point, but at that moment I was more concerned about losing my mind. Had she actually floated me off the line? Dodie said ghosts can't exert that kind of energy. If she hadn't floated me, why couldn't I remember moving forward? I would've had to have been completely off balance when I shot, but I felt nothing. I must have looked like a spaz out there!

Roxx viciously turned on Dodie. "She probably would have made that shot clean if you hadn't yelled from the bench! Way to go, Dodie!"

Karmyn nodded her head.

"What a dumb thing to do," CJ agreed as she applied deodorant.

I couldn't meet Dodie's eyes. I pretended I was struggling with a knot in my shoe.

"I'm not the one who broke her concentration," Dodie blurted out. She stood, looking taller than normal. "I think you have to tell them, Summer."

I met her eyes then, but with a look of incredulity. "What are you talking about, Dodie?" I asked with a weighted tone. I arched my eyebrows at her and gritted my teeth.

"She was there, right?" she confirmed. "At the end of the game?"

It was as if we stood, squaring off in an Old West movie.

Had Dodie become a traitor?

"Tell them about Coach Nola," Dodie said. "You have to, Summer. I saw how she affected you and the outcome of this game."

Karmyn cut in, "Now you sound like a lunatic, Dodie, not just a dodo!" It was the first time anyone had called her that to her face. The uncomfortable silence was broken by Roxx's snicker.

"Tell them, Summer," Dodie said, and she looked at me pleadingly.

"Well," I said, stalling, willing some lie to come into my head. "Well, I remembered what she said about walking onto the court as a winner at our last practice with her. That's what I was thinking when I went out and scored those baskets." I continued very carefully. "We should strive to remember that. When she named me captain, not everyone agreed, but I think I always give this team my full effort."

Everyone in the change room was nodding their heads except Dodie, who shook hers. "Tell them that Coach Nola's ghost is appearing and that you see her, Summer!"

"What?" Karmyn sliced through the silence, and everyone stared at me.

Dodie grew more defiant. "Remember at the séance? Roxx's attic?"

"We were just goofing around," Roxx stated, looking nervous. "Right?"

I had been getting the hang of lying, but at that moment, the knack seemed to elude me. I stammered, "I…I, well, I have seen her…I think."

Dodie nodded and took over. "We're trying to determine why Coach is appearing and why Summer is the only one who can see her." She paused as if an idea had struck. "Or maybe one of you has seen her as well but hasn't told anyone else." She looked around the room.

"Don't look at me!" declared Roxx. She scrunched her face

and twiddled her fingers like she was casting a spell. "Just because my grandmother held séances doesn't mean I'm in touch with the hoogly-booglies myself!"

Giggles relieved some of the tension in the room, but Dodie wouldn't stop. "I think she contributed to Summer violating at the line in today's game. I don't know how, because I don't even believe in ghosts, but I do know that Summer has never stepped over before, not once, not even in practice. Straight up. Straight down. That's how Summer always shoots."

"You're just trying to deflect the heat from yourself, Dodie. Dirk is furious with you!"

I said quietly, "It wasn't Dodie's fault that I missed. She was there. Coach Nola was under the hoop when I shot the final free throw. I don't know what she wants. I think she wants us to win, so I don't understand why I screwed up."

"The shot would only have tied the game," Val reminded everyone.

"We'd have won in overtime," Karmyn insisted. "We had momentum on our side! The Spartans were scrambling." She was repeating Coach Rogers' words from the post-game meeting. "And Dodie, here, knows that. Dodie, who never contributed at all to today's game and is now looking for a way to be the centre of attention." Karmyn was summarizing like a prosecutor in a courtroom. She circled Dodie as she spoke.

I repeated, "Dodie did not affect my shot!"

Karmyn continued, "And Summer, I don't really get why you're going along with all this, except maybe to cover for the fact that if you'd made that shot, we would have won. Weird that you'd make up a stupid story just to defend your miss! Or are you both really off your rockers? I wonder what the sports editor of the Garvin Weekly will write as his headline. *Poltergeist Wreaks Havoc at the Foul Line.*"

Dodie cut in with a panicky edge to her voice. "Obviously you can't tell anyone about this. Other people are not going to believe it."

"*Other* people?" Roxx demanded and then laughed with her head thrown way back.

I walked over to Dodie meaningfully. "Okay, Dodie, let's drop it. They didn't fall for it this time, either! You guys are way too savvy! Anyway, I'm sorry I screwed up the shot. I guess I was just exhausted. I couldn't believe I did that, just like you guys didn't believe our little hoax. We were just trying to keep Coach Nola's spirit alive, but really, Coach Rogers is doing a great job. We don't need two coaches, that's for sure." I was prattling like an idiot, anything to keep Karmyn from spreading the story. I was suddenly furious with Dodie. What if this got out? I'd become the laughingstock of the school.

"So, now there is no ghost? No ghost, right?" CJ sighed with relief and turned her attention to her bag and the search for a hairbrush.

"There's no ghost," I said. "I swear it."

Everyone looked to Dodie to confirm this, but she stared at me, adjusting her glasses and chewing the inside of her cheek.

"Well?" CJ insisted, brushing out her hair.

Dodie shrugged in response and met CJ's gaze with a believe-whatever-you-want expression. She peeled off her shoes, which still looked as if they'd never been worn, and shoved them into her bag.

"I don't get you two at all," Roxx muttered. Shaking her head, she added, "You are a pair of the biggest losers I have ever met. Good thing you have each other."

Faith, who'd been silent the whole time, finally said, "When's our next game?"

"This Tuesday," Karmyn answered. "Hope you won't be too scared to play, Summer."

I laughed as if Karmyn had made the funniest joke I'd ever heard. The rest of the girls finished changing their clothes. Val made sure she wasn't left alone in the change room, stumbling out next to the twins with her shoe laces left untied. I jammed my gear into my bag and thought about my family waiting for me out in the gym with who-knows-what-looks on their faces. Pity? Pride? Disappointment? Concern? How could I face them after this? I wanted to strangle Dodie. As the last of the girls exited the change room, I turned to where she'd been standing to tell her exactly what I thought of her, but she wasn't there. I swallowed hard and felt as if my fury could choke me. Tears seared my eyelids and spilled heat down my face.

"Thanks a lot, Dodie," I shouted into the empty room, and it echoed off the shower walls. "I hate you so much!"

There was a sudden sound as if someone had opened the change room door. When I whirled around to see who was there, the door swung shut, and then there was nothing but dead silence.

CHAPTER TWENTY

Food can be comforting. Especially Italian food. Must be all the carbs. It had been a quite a while since the bad feelings in my stomach had left room for a good meal. I'd told Mom and Dad after the game that I wasn't hungry.

"Nonsense!" Dad had insisted. "By the time we drive to the restaurant, you'll be ravenous after exerting that kind of energy."

"The Italian Eatery is your favourite," Mom reminded me.

Everett seemed to act on their cue and rubbed his tummy, adding, "We're starved just from watching. That was huge, Summer. You got game, girl."

Holly was the only one who tried a different tack. "Tough one at the end," she murmured to me.

Mom shot her a stern look as we piled into the car and drove to the restaurant.

The Eatery is a family-owned restaurant with red-and-white checkered tablecloths and a colour-changing fountain with filters that turn the water red, then green, then blue, as it pours out of the goddess statue's urn. When you enter, the waft of fresh garlic and oregano starts you salivating at the door. I ate a plateful of fettuccini Alfredo, three breadsticks and a Caesar salad, washing it down with two Shirley Temples and endless ice water. Dad asked the owner, Mr. Rizzono, to recommend his best gelato for dessert, and I finished a bowl of that, too. After I stopped long enough to breathe, I accidentally belched aloud, and instead of Mom giving me a reproving look, she laughed and snorted into her napkin. This set the whole table off into gales of laughter. We remained there long after our meal had been cleared away and the other patrons had gone home. At times, all you could hear was the bubbling of the fountain, the speaker emitting muted Italian opera and our sighs of contentment. The Eatery felt like an island in paradise that night. My eyelids drooped from the warmth and humidity. My mind drifted…floated…

Fiery metal sizzled as it hit the cold, dark ocean waves. Coach Nola's sad eyes peered through the depths.

"Aaahhh!??" I sat up, sputtering.

Mom was out of her chair and suddenly holding me by the shoulders. "Summer, are you okay?" she asked, staring into my eyes.

"Yeah, I dozed off, didn't I?"

Mom nodded, but the crease in her forehead stayed as she took her own seat again. There was a split second when I thought everyone was looking at everyone else with the same concern, but then Dad pulled some coins out of his pocket and said, "As soon as the kids finish their espresso, we'll call it a night. In the meantime, Summer, go make a wish."

"A wish?" I asked, feeling as if I was resurfacing.

"Are you sure you're all right, Summer?" Mom asked again.

"Fine. I'm fine," I said, trying to shake off the sucking pressure. "I'm just tired," I said and yawned, but my whole body shuddered. The eyes had frightened me.

Dad put the coins in my hand. I closed my fist around their hard weight. A wish was such a tall order, wasn't it? What would I wish for? And would what I wished for come true? For Coach to stop haunting me? For Karmyn and Roxx to cease being so mean? For Dodie to have never told the team about the ghost sightings? For a win in our next game? For a win at the Provincial Championship? For a second chance to tie tonight's game? For Coach Nola to still be alive?

"I might have to empty out your bank account, Dad, before I can finish wishing," I muttered under my breath. I tossed the coins all at once in a shower of silver. The colour filter changed the water to blue as a dozen tiny splashes rippled across the fountain's surface.

"Careful what you wish for," Everett joked from the table.

Holly punched him in the arm.

"I was just saying," Everett mewed pathetically, rubbing the wounded spot. He was so melodramatic we couldn't help but laugh. I had to hold my stomach. It was beginning to ache. I forgot to wish.

As I excused myself to go to the washroom, I overheard Holly hiss at Everett. "Don't say something that's going to make her start crying again!"

I paused at the bathroom door where they couldn't see me.

"She was crying?" Everett asked innocently.

"Before she came out of the change room," Holly confirmed.

"You mean over the last shot?"

Mom cleared her throat. The discussion ended.

Poor Everett, I thought. His favourite pastime is making people laugh, and my sister is accusing him of making me cry. Holly was acting weird. Still, it made me feel good inside to know she cared enough to try to protect me. By the time I returned to the table, they had their coats on, and Dad was paying the bill. He was also bragging to Mr. Rizzono that his youngest daughter had scored over twenty points in her basketball game that night.

"Good! Much success, no? Mr. Rizzono said and smiled so wide that his gold tooth gleamed.

"Thank you," I said, feeling the blood rushing into my cheeks. "And that was the best food ever!" I added, hoping Dad wouldn't continue.

Mr. Rizzono called after us, "You come back soon. Bring your team for pizza!"

"Good idea," Mom said with an attempt at merriment. "That would be fun!"

The whole family was acting weird. Poor Everett might

run away screaming soon. Didn't he have enough strained intensity with his own parents? I turned to him and said, "Thanks a lot for coming to my game tonight. It was so cool to see you and Holly in the bleachers."

"Hey, I can't wait for the next time I can make it out. And Baxter's got a home game in a couple of weeks. We'll all go to that."

"Super!" I said. In a couple of weeks…in a couple of weeks… Oh, if only things would be super in a couple of weeks.

There was a soft tap on my bedroom door as I lay in my bed, staring at the half moon outside my window. Holly shuffled in, wearing her fleece nightie with the pink lambs and blue clouds. She pushed me over and crawled under the covers, smelling of apple hair conditioner and magnolia moisturizer, which lured me into a comfort zone.

"So what happened out there, Summer?"

"Out where?" I asked cautiously.

"At the foul line tonight."

"What do you mean?" I tugged to take back my share of the quilt.

Holly tugged back. "Mom's worried, Summer. And now I'm worried. You've been acting so strange…getting into trouble at school, disappearing into your room instead of joining into conversation, falling asleep at the restaurant tonight…and having a nightmare."

"Hey, I'd just played really hard. And I couldn't fall asleep last night because of your music."

"Summer, you snuck out of the house last night. My music was turned off by nine-thirty."

My heart thudded. "Did you tell Mom?"

"No. I figured you were probably meeting a boy."

I sighed with relief.

She continued, "A boy who maybe isn't the best influence on you? Was he at the game tonight? Is that why you kinda lost your concentration?"

"Jeez, it's like I committed a criminal offence because I flubbed the shot," I said and tried to turn my shoulder away.

"The shot went in, Summer, but something else happened. You went all weird. Almost as if you saw...oh, I don't know."

I swallowed hard and licked my lips. Was she about to say *a ghost*? Icy fingers tracked my spine and I shivered even though Holly's body heat was turning the bed into a sauna.

"Summer," she said, sighing. "Mom thinks there's something wrong. She thinks you might have had a *petit mal*."

"What the heck is that?" I said, and was suddenly very still.

"It's a kind of small epileptic seizure. Not the kind most people think about when you say the word *seizure*. It's like a moment lost in time to the person experiencing it. Like your brain disconnects for a moment and you're not aware of what's going on around you. That didn't happen, did it?"

I didn't answer.

"Do you think that's what happened, Summer?"

"Did Mom send you to find out, Holly?"

"No. Mom would kill me if she knew I was saying this to you, because she doesn't want you to think there's something wrong if there really isn't. Dad is assuring her that you were just tired, that you've never had to play so hard before, and that allows Mom to be content with denial. But I think that's ridiculous. If there's something wrong, we should find out."

"There's nothing wrong," I said.

"Summer, your denial will just add to the problem, if there is one."

"I'm not having seizures!" I insisted.

"Ssshhh," Holly warned. "Then there's a guy, isn't there?" she said smugly, as if she was right again – as if she was the one in the family who never got into trouble.

"No, there's no guy either!" I said through clenched teeth.

"Oh, come on, Summer," she said. "Fess up. I promise I won't tell."

"There is no boy!"

"Just tell me his initials."

I just wanted Holly to be wrong for once. I blurted, "I'm... I'm seeing Coach Nola."

"What?" Holly said, as if she hadn't heard me.

"I saw...I saw Coach Nola when I was trying to shoot."

"You what?" Holly shrieked and then covered her mouth. She moved away from me as if she was suddenly in danger of being infected with something. Then she took a breath and said, "Summer, Ms. Blythe died at Christmas."

"I know she died, Holly. I'm not crazy," I insisted.

"Then what are you saying?" she said, as if she wished with all her heart that I hadn't said any of it.

"The team had a séance. I didn't want to, but they said I was chicken and wouldn't be on the team." The words were tumbling out now, telling Holly the whole story, even Dodie's theories, and ending with "But you can't tell anyone. Dodie told the other girls tonight, and I'm afraid it'll spread like wildfire. I'll be the laughingstock of the world. But I'm sure she's really there, Holly. I smell coconut, and then she's there, and I don't know why."

Holly was dazed when she answered. "She was in the tropics when she died."

I nodded. "I know."

"That's why you smell the coconuts, Summer."

"What?" I said, confused.

"Well, that part seems obvious to me," Holly said. "Not that I'm saying I believe any of this."

"I know. Most of the time I try and convince myself that I don't believe it, either. If I don't believe it, then how can it happen again? I didn't think it was going to happen again. Then tonight it did!"

Holly started scrunching her short cropped hair so hard

that I thought she might pull a handful right out. "This is crazy. My baby sister thinks she's seeing a ghost."

The tears started spilling down my face. It was horrible to see the effect my words were having on my sister. "You can't tell Mom and Dad, Holly. Swear you won't tell them!"

Holly hugged me so hard, I couldn't breathe. "We'll figure something out, Summer. Don't worry, don't worry," she repeated. But it sounded like she was trying to convince herself.

CHAPTER TWENTY-ONE

Cognitive and General Psychological Assessment
Brain Injury and Neurological Illness
Post-Accident/Incident Trauma
Abuse/Grief Issues
Depression/Anxiety/Self-Esteem
Stress/Anger Management
ADHD Learning Disabilities
Phobias/Panic Attacks
Eating Disorders
Behaviour Problems

I sat in the waiting room of the offices of Jackson, Jillhart & Janworski, Registered Psychologists, reading the brochures for their Children and Adolescent Services, wondering under what category they would place me, and also wondering if your name had to start with a *J* to be allowed to practise there. My mom kept patting my knee. Perhaps that's because I was fidgeting in my chair, and the only other people in the waiting room – a mother in a pink Chanel-style suit and her tattooed, Goth-style daughter – were glancing and glaring at us respectively.

I sat and planted both my feet on the floor, and for the hundredth time wished that Holly would either break out in an itchy rash from head to toe or be hospitalized for malaria. Her inability to keep a secret had resulted in five straight hours of parental grilling, phone calls to the school that I would not be returning until further notice (please have her school work left at the office for pick-up and notify her basketball coach), a complete and thorough medical examination, an MRI scan booked for the following week (as a favour to Mom, Mrs. Direland pulled some strings at her previous hospital, taking advantage of a cancellation there), plus this – a psychological assessment. If I didn't have a psychological problem before, I certainly had one now, but was there a treatment for mortification? How could I ever return to school? Dodie, Karmyn and Roxx would be having a field day informing everyone why I wasn't attending. If I ever did go back, I'd be labelled as a nut-case. Kids would give me a wide berth in the halls and be afraid of sitting anywhere near me in the cafeteria in case I infected their food.

When the other mom and daughter were called into one of the offices and we were alone in the waiting room, Mom started again with possible explanations. "Like I said, Summer, the ghost you're seeing could be a kind of aura that migraine sufferers often experience."

"I don't get a headache when I see…it." Mom had insisted I call the ghost "it" in discussions with the doctors. "Do auras have eyes?"

Mom treated that as a rhetorical question. Her only answer was to squirm in her chair a bit.

"And if it's an aura, then what am I doing here?"

"Dr. Glovell thought it wouldn't hurt to talk with someone."

I sighed. "I'm tired of talking," I muttered.

"With a professional," Mom added.

I crossed my arms and gritted my teeth. When we were called into Dr. Jillhart's office, I realized that just because I'd been referred there, didn't mean I had to cooperate. Why would I want to tell some stranger about seeing Coach Nola? So they could lock me away? It would be better to just sit there and not say a word. This strategy was easier than I expected due to the fact that once I saw Dr. Jillhart, I didn't want to talk to him anyway. He had a long, scraggly beard that drooped over his creased shirt. His tie was too short. He peered at me with an expression that made me wonder if his eyeglass prescription was strong enough. As I sat silent and defiant, Mom was forced to answer his endless questions, everything from did I enjoy school to had I experienced menses yet? This got me wondering if I only saw Coach Nola when I had my period. But no, that wasn't the case.

Mom nudged my ankle a lot and gave me very stern looks. I could see she was both bewildered and embarrassed by my behaviour, and this made me feel slightly guilty. But I resented being made to feel guilty, and that fuelled my determination to maintain zipped lips. Mom filled the awkward silences, but she also resorted to her own maternal psychology, "How is Dr. Jillhart supposed to help you, Summer?"

I shrugged.

"You told your dad and me that you wanted whatever was happening to stop. Dr. Jillhart may be able to help, but not if you won't talk about it."

Dr. Jillhart puffed his chest out a bit at that moment and then let his breath out slowly, the same technique Mrs. Chamber used to calm herself. He chose his next words carefully, twiddling his pen, trying to look nonchalant. "Summer, there is one question I want to pose – the answer to which I personally don't know." He cleared his throat. "What exactly is a ghost? In *your* opinion?"

I scratched my head and chewed on the inside of my cheek. Mom nudged my ankle a little harder than before. Dr. Jillhart ran his hand down his abbreviated tie, checked his watch and waited. We could hear the traffic outside the heavily curtained window; someone's car alarm was going off in the parking lot below.

I finally said, "I re-al-ly don't know."

"Summer!" Mom said in exasperation.

Dr. Jillhart waved his hand to placate Mom and then

smiled and nodded. "Well, Summer, if you don't mind just stepping out into the waiting room, I'll have a few words with your mother and then you can both be on your way."

My victory was short-lived. Mom barged out of his office. She marched me into the elevator and when the doors closed, she said, "Summer, your uncooperative behaviour was not amusing! Dr. Jillhart was trying to help you."

I shrugged.

"If this proves to be a mental health concern, we are not sweeping it under the carpet." She sighed and said, "I just hope you'll be a little more talkative at your next appointment with the psychiatrist."

"The *psychiatrist*? He thinks I'm crazy?"

"He feels you might benefit from talking to a doctor with some experience in psychoanalysis. He's recommended someone."

I felt very ashamed. "I'm not crazy!" I yelled as the doors slid open. A woman who was waiting shifted over to the next elevator without looking at us.

Mom was on the verge of tears. "I wish you had started talking in the office, Summer."

We drove home in silence. What was wrong with me? The question seemed to be growing exponentially.

CHAPTER TWENTY-TWO

It seemed there was no end to the guilt I could accumulate. Mom and Dad stopped speaking to each other for two whole days over whether or not I should see a psychiatrist. Dad won a partial victory when Mom agreed to wait until after my MRI scan was completed, but she was so angry, she snatched his dinner plate and scraped it into the garbage before he was half finished. Dad left the house in a huff even though it was almost forty below and his car engine barely turned over. Holly spent the evening crying in her room, and when Dad finally came home close to midnight, Holly wailed that Everett had decided to stay away for a while until things were sorted out at our house. "Sounds a little too tense" was what he'd said. If I'd been communicating with anyone at that time, I would have labelled that an understatement, but I figured that the easiest thing was to pretend I was sleeping a lot and give monosyllabic grunts in response to most of the questions posed to me. That took less energy than having to describe over and over again what I'd seen and having Mom diagnose a dozen unlikely medical explanations for it.

My teachers sent home little notes along with my homework saying they hoped I would be feeling better and returning soon. The phone never rang. I reasoned that my status at school had gone far beyond loser to certified *nutcase*. Every time I thought about walking back into the hallways of Garvin Junior High, my brain felt as if it were housing an ant colony, an endless stream of fidgeting, sustenance-seeking, ravenous insects swarming over and through the grey matter until I was ready to scream. To make it stop, I'd wrap my pillow around my head and bang it against the wall. Mom scurried around muttering words like *autism* and *impossibility*. Dad would sometimes pick me right up and rock me in the rocking chair like a baby. My legs were so long that they dangled on the floor. Holly continued to cry a lot and started wringing her hands like Lady Macbeth. It was evident that I was like a low-pressure front carrying a storm into the midst of my own family.

Everyone seemed genuinely relieved on the morning of my MRI scan. Except me. Would the specialists discover that bugs had literally invaded my brain? Or that a tumour pressed on my optic nerves, causing the apparitions? Or was it possible they might see Nola Blythe in there for themselves – her energy pulsing in sectors of my head in the same way it scrambled the scoreboard? The sky was a bright clear blue as we drove into Winnipeg, so bright it hurt my eyes. Two sundogs had formed on either side of the sun, a rainbow reminder that it was still forty below outside despite the sun's attempt to warm the invading arctic wind.

A nurse in a white lab coat handed Mom a clipboard with a sheet of personal medical information to fill out for me. It required her signature of consent for the procedure to commence. Dad sat forward on his vinyl chair with his elbows resting on his knees, his hands clasped out in front of him. The receptionist shuffled files and answered what seemed like endless telephone calls. I had a view of the parking lot, and I tried to focus on the cars that came and went, and I wondered what all the people were coming and going for.

A nurse pivoted on her silent shoes and looked at me.

"Summer Widden? Hi, Summer. I'm Amy," she chirped. "We're ready to take some pictures now."

Another white-coated woman invited me to lie down on a gurney. She didn't introduce herself the way Amy did. Instead, she referred to her clipboard and told me what I could expect in the next twenty minutes or so. Every so often, she paused, flipped a page over, and asked me again if I'd ever had any other serious health problems. As she wheeled me into a smaller white room where the MRI machine was housed, she said, smiling, "You'll have to remain very, very still. Do you think you can do that? You're not the jittery type, are you? Ants in your pants?"

I wanted to tell her that, recently, there had been an entire colony invading my brain, but I knew that wasn't the brightest idea. At least the insects hadn't eaten away all of my ability to think. Not yet. But every so often, I found myself not being able to understand what she was saying. I focused on her straight, white teeth but couldn't understand the words her lips were forming. I had to strain to concentrate again. I had fleeting images of Coach Nola's beautiful white teeth before she died.

Amy smiled. "Just try and relax, Summer. I'm going to take your blood pressure before we begin."

As she did this, the technician explained, "There will be some loud banging noises. That's normal. It's just the machine doing its job. Try to ignore the noise, relax and remember to remain very, very still. I'll be in the other room and you'll be able to hear my voice. Press this little buzzer if for some reason you feel you can't continue. And as soon as I've switched off the machine, I'll be right here to take you out."

With that, they wheeled me into the white tunnel of the machine. At first, relaxing was easy. It was as if they'd slid me into a white-puffed marshmallow with a hole scooped out just for me. But then the noise started. I'd been warned one final time about it as the nurses exited the room, but the hollow drum beat booming and buzzing made me twitch, and that in turn made me think I wasn't staying still enough, and that caused me to be tense and try to hold my breath better, and that in turn made me dizzy and panicky at the same time. I couldn't think of anything except when would it be over? When they finally wheeled me out of the magnetic marshmallow monster, their voices cheerful and full of praise for how well I'd done, I broke down and sobbed. The technician went to fetch my parents, and Dad started into a long-winded explanation about how the MRI machine actually works, and how there was nothing for me to worry about. Mom rubbed my back and tried to hush Dad, and Amy murmured to Mom that she wondered if a sedative might be useful. Mom snapped a no at her, which made me sob even harder because Amy had been so sweet. I bawled all the way home. Dad carried me to my room and put me to bed, and I heard Mom outside the door wondering aloud if a sedative might have been a good idea after all. Dad stood in the doorway, removed his wired-together glasses and ran his hand over his face the way he would if we'd been camping for a week and he hadn't shaved for the entire trip. He guided Mom away from the door and down the hall.

They left me alone with my thoughts, which weren't very good company. I resented everyone: my parents, Holly, and especially Dodie. I could never go back to school again because of Dodie Direland. And I would never play basketball again because of her.

That's when I caught a whiff of coconut. I raised my head, swiping tears out of my eyes so that I could see. My desk lamp seemed to flicker, pulse, dim. My heart thudded so hard that my last sob sounded like a strangled hiccup. Coach Nola appeared as if someone had switched her on. I had never witnessed her actual appearance from thin air before; she had been waiting for me to turn and notice her in previous sightings, but this time, she just materialized while I stared. My mini-hoop basketball rolled off the desk and under my bed. She turned her vacant eyes toward my framed team picture, and her hand seemed to pass right through it… And then she was gone.

I tried to call out to my parents to tell them that she'd come and gone, but my throat constricted into a narrow reed that allowed only the thinnest squeak to escape. My alarm clock read 5:30 p.m. Game time. The Garvin Invaders were scheduled to be playing a divisional game at that very moment. The longing to be there cut through me like a knife. I didn't want to be rolled into machines with giant magnets that took pictures of my brain; I wanted to be normal again, playing basketball and walking home through the snow. I grabbed my alarm clock and threw it at the spot where Coach Nola had appeared. It knocked my team picture flying, and I heard the crack of its glass frame. Mom and Dad came running. Mom's face seemed to cave in on itself; she let out a tiny sound that resembled a stifled chuckle, but what followed was the wail of a wounded animal. Dad bent down to pick up the shards of glass. Holly dashed down the hall and when she braked at the doorway and took in the scene, I heard her mutter above Mom's wailing, "Maybe we need an exorcism." They settled on a sleeping pill, a sedative, which the doctor on call at Garvin Hospital ordered for me. I slept a dreamless sleep.

CHAPTER TWENTY-THREE

"Where are we going?" I asked Holly.

"You'll see," she replied, checking the rear-view mirror before changing lanes.

I crossed my arms and gripped my elbows with my mittened hands. "I refuse to go to mediums, fortune tellers, new age shops, witch doctors or exorcists. That includes counselling services as well," I added.

Holly shot me an exasperated look and said in a condescending tone, "You're pretty picky for someone who could use any or all of those services."

I jerked my head away and stared out the passenger window. It was early Saturday morning. Traffic was light. There was a shimmering layer of hoarfrost coating the outside world. The sun glinted off it, transforming tree branches into sparkling strands of diamonds.

My tongue seemed coated with ice crystals, too. "I'm not talking to anybody else about what's happened to me, Holly. I should never have told you! No one would be poking and prodding and referring me to shrinks!"

"Oh, no," Holly admonished. "You'd just continue breaking and entering, skipping classes, smashing things, seeing ghosts, and no one would take the least notice, Summer. Everyone would just call it a teenage phase or something. No one would bother you while you went insane."

"Oh, shut up, Holly," I muttered and cranked the knob on the car heater to full blast. I was sick of everyone thinking

I was mentally unsound.

Holly had to raise her voice to be heard over the heater fan. "Oh, and did I mention you would continue to be really nasty as well?"

"Maybe you'd be nasty too, if you were the one seeing the ghost!" I was arguing just to win now, spitting the words out.

"Maybe I'd admit I needed help if I was the one seeing the ghost!" Holly responded, braking hard at a red light.

I bit my tongue as we fishtailed on the slippery road, narrowly missing the car in the lane next to us. Holly took a deep breath and unwound the fluffy scarf from around her neck before cautiously accelerating on the green light.

After a moment I muttered, "That's because you don't believe she's there, but she is, and that scares all the rest of you to death, doesn't it?"

Holly clamped her mouth shut and sniffed again, concentrating on her driving.

I took the opportunity to taunt her. "You're not sure what scares you most, a crazy sister or an honest-to-goodness haunting ghost."

Holly sighed and then said in a small voice, "And you're not sure either, Summer. To ward off your own fear, you work yourself into a rage. You saw her in your bedroom last night, didn't you?"

I continued to stare out the window. The glistening brightness seared my eyes, and my eyelids felt as if they were weighted with lead – the after-effect of the previous night's sleeping pill.

After a moment's silence, Holly said, "This was Everett's idea. He's worried about you, too."

Sometimes the sympathy of a stranger or near-stranger can be more overwhelming than your own family's. My throat closed tight shut, and my need to fight Holly was choked out of me. I said quietly, "I thought he didn't want to come around until I was *cured*."

Holly couldn't keep the happiness off her face. "I misunderstood what he said. He just didn't want to be in the way or a nuisance to anyone. In the end, he personally fought Mom on this one. Good thing Dad agreed or we wouldn't be here."

Holly turned off Main Street and parked next to the university's athletic centre. "Actually, you can thank Baxter and Baxter's coach as much as Everett." She reached into the back seat and tossed my gym bag into my lap. I hadn't even noticed it was there. "Here's your stuff," Holly continued. "Baxter said to be prepared to refill your water bottle. You can thank me for finding a clean t-shirt that matches your shorts." With her final comment, she pulled off her glove and scrutinized her fingernails in an exaggerated diva gesture.

Inside the Buffalo Centre, one basketball court was partitioned off from the others, and Baxter and Everett were standing at the three-point line, shooting a rackful of balls at the hoop. From the other court, I could hear the intense sounds of play – dribbling, squeaking shoes, men shouting, the coach shouting louder. "Here, here, here! Shoot! Shoot! Dead ball. Cut through! Cut through! How many times did we run that drill? Take that shot when you see him sag off! Am *I* supposed to get that rebound? Then *who* is supposed to get that rebound?"

Everett's voice overrode the commotion on the next court. "Hey, Summer. You made it!" He waved and hustled over. "This is my brother, Baxter."

Baxter followed behind Everett. He wiped his sweaty hand down the front of his even sweatier Agassiz U t-shirt and offered it apologetically. We shook. My hand looked like one of those unstretched mini gloves next to Baxter's huge mitt of a hand. After we shook, he tapped his fist to his chest and said, "Honoured to meet you."

It was a strange little gesture. It was as if he was saying he knew that everyone thought I was a nutcase, but it didn't bother him.

My mouth hung open for a moment before I could muster,

"I'm the one who's honoured. I saw you in the game against Assiniboine U!"

"Thanks," he said and started to spin a ball on his finger while Everett took over the talking.

"We thought you might feel like a practice since you're not at school right now. Baxter's coach said he could be excused from the final hour of his practice. One hour. That's all we've got. Women's locker room is that red door on the right. It's propped open for you."

I changed faster than I could ever remember. The after-effects of the sleeping pill seemed to vanish. When I sprang out of the locker room, Holly was nestled in the stands with a college text and Baxter called out over the adjoining court melee, "Three times around the perimeter, then come in for some stretching."

My feet barely touched the hardwood. The gym was huge and the air pungent with sweat. I felt as if I'd been invited to paradise. There was a rack of women's balls just for me. While Baxter made me dribble through pylons, shoot 'round-the-world at least thirty times, and then drive in, layup, drive in, layup, drive in, layup over and over again, I never once thought of my problems.

"Water break," Everett called for the third time and staggered off the court to flop down beside Holly.

I wiped my face with the bottom of my t-shirt. Even Coach Nola had never worked me this hard. My legs felt a little like jelly and my shoulders ached. I sat down on the hardwood and glanced at the scoreboard. It was switched off, no score, no fouls. I held my breath to see if it would suddenly come to life, but it remained a black blank. I gulped water and closed my eyes in gratitude.

"Tired?"

My eyes flashed open. Baxter was standing over me. I nodded.

"Good," he said. "That's good." He flashed me a huge smile.

I felt my knees weaken even more, and a slow crimson that

had nothing to do with exhaustion crept into my cheeks. I wiped my face again, hoping I could hide my blushing from Baxter.

"You're a good hard worker, Summer," he said, and eased his long body down beside me.

I smiled back at him, trying not to seem thrilled about the compliment, even though I felt as if someone had lit me from the inside.

He continued, "Work ethic is a huge part of this game. Your skills are pretty darn good, too. Nola Blythe must have been quite a coach to bring you this far."

"She was," I said, and for the first time in a long while, I felt a rush of gratitude toward her instead of an uneasy fear.

"Was she fun?" Baxter asked as he lay down on his back and stretched his quads.

"Yes, she always made it fun," I said. "Not fun as in silly ha-ha, but fun because...well, because she was always so excited about the game."

"Yeah, good coaches do that," Baxter said, switching legs.

"She really wanted to win," I added.

"Good coaches want that, too," Baxter said. "And great coaches, I think, find a way to keep the word 'sport' in sports, if that makes any sense."

"It does," I responded.

Baxter folded both legs into a yoga position and then pressed his knees down toward the floor. He continued, "I had a coach once who preached, 'Don't play for me. You have to play for yourself.' But I know I play for my coaches. I know I play better for the coaches I really respect and admire – and unfortunately, vice versa. I still have a couple of coaches who won't leave my head because even though I'm playing here on a university team, I can't help feeling I still need to prove something to them."

"Why not send them a ticket to one of your games?" I suggested.

Baxter smirked at me.

"No, really!" I insisted. "The thing is that those coaches probably never made it this far in the sport, right? You're better now than they could ever be."

He stopped stretching and pushed a hand through his short hair, rubbing it so that it stood on end. He muttered, "Who is supposed to be helping whom, here?"

Under my breath, I added, "I think it would be fun to see the look on their faces."

Baxter heard me and stood. "Fun! Now you're talking! Fun is the *key* point! No pun intended. When it stops being fun, it's time to quit. Are you having fun here?"

I nodded enthusiastically.

"Then it's not time to quit! Ready? Let's work on some passing with our last few minutes. And Summer, as long as it's fun, don't let anything – not anything, not anyone – keep you from that."

I nodded, though I wanted to tell him how impossible that seemed in my present situation. I tugged at my socks and sighed.

He broke into my thoughts."Hey, on your feet, Lazybones. We're going to work on some passing now." He contorted his face into the meanest coach face imaginable, and a split second later, he chuckled as I scrambled to my feet.

We both laughed as we passed the ball up and down the court, up and down, up and down, up and down.

"But, Mom," Holly insisted, "you should have seen her!"

I stood in the bathroom, towel-drying my hair and straining to hear Holly's argument.

"It was just like the old Summer. She was so happy. You have to let her go back and start playing again."

"But what if this is all a result of her taking that blow to the head from the ball in the change room? I wish she'd told us about that when it happened instead of my finding out after Dodie admitted it to her mother."

I couldn't see Mom, but I imagined she was wringing her hands and looking ten years older than she was. Another pang of guilt swept over me, but it was countered as I wondered if Dodie was going to continue to be one big gushing faucet of information and ruin my life even more than she had already.

Holly persisted. "And what if the hit to the head had nothing to do with it? What if it's her grief, some post-traumatic stress, and she just needs time to work through it? Keeping her prisoner at home is only going to make matters worse. She needs to be playing basketball."

Mom's voice grew stern. "Look, Holly, I love Everett. Your father and I are very happy he's part of your life. And we're sure Baxter is just as fine a person, but isn't he just a first-year student? That doesn't give him psychologist credentials."

I held my breath. I'd forgotten that Everett had told me that Baxter wanted to be a sports psychologist. Was there an ulterior motive to my basketball lesson? Was it just another shrink session? "Keep-it-fun" therapy? He'd worked me awfully hard for it to be nothing but fun. My quads ached from running and jumping, my shoulders from shooting. I wanted to discredit my suspicious thoughts when suddenly his phrase about the coaches who wouldn't leave his head came flooding over me. Was he comparing my ghost to his own hauntings? Was he suggesting I needed to prove something to Coach Nola? Prove that I could live up to her expectations of me? And because she died, I couldn't prove it…unless *I* brought her back to life…unless *I* created her ghost there at court-side. How could I ever fulfill her expectations? *It's not whether you win or lose, but how you win the game.* Would she haunt me forever? If I was creating her, then the best way to *uncreate* her was to quit playing basketball.

CHAPTER TWENTY-FOUR

The MRI results came back perfectly normal. This seemed to upset my mother more than if they'd found something wrong. For her, an actual treatable medical condition – even one in my brain – would have been preferable to the nebulous psychological conundrum that my ghost-sighting presented. After all, people walked into the hospital with all kinds of broken parts and left with them repaired. Those kinds of conditions were familiar to Mom; she dealt with them every day. A haunting was not familiar territory and had her sitting in the living room staring into the fireplace, rousing herself only long enough to take good long looks at me before retreating back to the hearth. She no longer seemed very certain about a cure.

Dad, on the other hand, was immensely relieved. Once he found out I didn't have a brain tumour, he thought he could cajole me out of whatever it was that had me spooked. He bought a brand spanking new DVD player and a flat-screen, surround-sound entertainment system and rented dozens of his favourite comedies. Steve Martin, Adam Sandler, Whoopi Goldberg, Billy Crystal and Bette Midler moved into our living room and drove Mom away from her fireside brooding. Holly came in occasionally to inform Dad that he should think about my starting school again, but she would become involved in whatever was on the big screen and forget to push her argument.

Watching the videos day and night was like an endless loop of recess. I didn't have to deal with my problems. I just submerged myself in one-liners, absurdity, and madcap mayhem. For that, I was thankful to my dad. At least, until it was time to turn the system off and go to bed. Then I had to think about the inevitable. My having to go back to school was fast approaching. I could just imagine the crowded hallways parting to let Summer-the-crazy-girl-who-sees-ghosts through.

The worst part, though, would be walking past the gym. I knew if I told Mom that I was far behind in my school work and had no time for basketball, she would be delighted to inform Principal Talbot that I was not going to continue on the team. It was me I didn't trust. How could I pass by and not start longing for the feel of the ball in my hand, the *whack* on the backboard as the ball bounced off on its way through the hoop, the smell of sweaty jerseys and sneakers? Being on the court in the Buffalo Centre with Baxter and Everett had been like visiting heaven. I could already feel acid-green jealousy creeping over my skin at the thought of Karmyn and Roxx and the others on the court without me. Coach Nola hadn't appeared in two weeks; maybe she wasn't coming back. But could I take the chance?

"Dad," I began after hitting the pause button on the DVD player. Martin Short froze on the screen and provided the only light in the living room. I continued. "I've been thinking. I really don't want to go back to school this year. Junior high is way too stressful. Everyone's so mean there and now that the whole school knows I saw a ghost, they'll think I'm bonkers. I'd really like to be home-schooled. You could do that, right? I would have fewer distractions. I'd learn way more than the kids in the classroom. I'd work really hard, maybe even skip a year and start university or college sooner."

Dad's expression altered from TV-screen mirth to consternation as I spoke. Part of his face was in shadow as he started to respond. "Summer, I teach electrical shop. I'm not current on algebra or social studies or any academic subjects."

"Other teachers switch around and teach new things in our school. You're way smart, Dad."

He turned and looked at me, adjusting his glasses. "Thank you, Summer." He paused before he countered with a weak defence. "But I'm in class all day. How would that work if you're home all day?"

"I know you would have to put in extra hours, but I'd take the initiative. Our teachers spend half their time reminding us to get to work, do the work, complete the work. I'd just *do* the work in the daytime and we could have brief lessons in the evening, so you could still tinker down in the basement with your radios and whatnot." I beamed at him.

He ran a hand over his scratchy whiskers. "I don't know, Summer. You'd have no social contact with kids your own age. That wouldn't be healthy."

"Just because I wouldn't be in school wouldn't mean I couldn't have slumber parties and stuff." I was starting to sound whiny. I knew Dad didn't go in for whiny, so I cleared my throat and said in the most mature voice I could muster, "Please consider home-schooling me, Dad. I think it would be...advantageous! Oh, and don't worry about French: I can take that by correspondence."

He half-sighed, half-grunted in response. "I'll talk to your mother," he said.

He reached over, took the remote from my hand and turned off the system. The room was plunged into darkness. We both sat still for a moment and listened to the hum of the furnace as it pumped heat through the vents.

Dad broke the spell with a voice that cracked partway through. "Your mother and I are willing to do whatever it takes to get you well."

I let out a deep breath. My plan was clinched. Or so I thought.

The next evening at dinner, Mom didn't eat anything on her plate. She sat with her back rigid as she spoke. "Dr. Jillhart – despite Summer's refusal to speak to him in the session we had – consulted with some psychiatric colleagues, bless his soul."

Dad cleared his throat and gave a Mom a meaningful glance. Mom relaxed a bit but avoided looking at me. She raised her fork, twiddling it while she continued. "Dr. Jillhart and the others feel that isolation would not be a recommended course of action at this point in time. They feel that the…episodes…were not psychotic in nature, therefore not directly harmful to you, Summer, or to those around you." She turned to me, put down the fork and rested her hands in her lap. "I mean, Dad and I didn't even know they were happening to you."

For a moment, she dropped her triage nurse image and slumped in her chair.

Dad cleared his throat. "What your mom is saying, what we're saying, Summer, is that we think you need to be back in school."

Holly nodded vigorously. "I agree!"

"I'm not going," I said, pushing my plate away.

"Summer, be reasonable," Dad said.

"I'm not going," I repeated.

"Now, listen, Summer…" Mom began.

"I'm not going back to school. Don't you understand I'm a freak now?"

"You're not a freak," Holly insisted.

"Oh, right," I said. "You're the one who wouldn't go to high school or junior high unless you were wearing three complete coats of mascara, just in case the fashion police arrived to examine your eyelashes. I see ghosts, Holly!"

"Now, listen, Summer," Mom said and gripped the edges of the dinner table. "There is no need to get off track and start attacking your sister. Your going back to school has nothing to do with Holly's mascara. And you *are* going back to school. End of discussion."

Dad sighed and rubbed the stubble on his cheeks again. "It's for the best right now," he said. "You need to give it a try."

Holly chimed in, "And it's an accepted fact that physical activity improves mental health, Summer, so you need to be playing basketball."

"NO!" I exclaimed, so forcefully that Dad's back straightened in his chair and he held his breath.

Holly scrunched her eyes at me. "After everything Baxter and Everett did for you? Do you know how privileged you were to have an entire university court to yourself?"

I clenched my teeth.

Dad raised his hand to shush Holly.

Mom patted my hand. "One thing at a time, Summer… although Dr. Jillhart did say he thought returning to sports was a good idea as well."

Dr. Jillhart this, Dr. Jillhart that! So I wasn't psychotic enough for Dr. Jillhart? I eyed my dinner plate. Suddenly I lunged for it and flipped it over. The remains of my meal flew across the table, splattering everyone. I shouted, "The ghost is going to return if you make me go back there. It'll serve you all right!" In a heartbeat I was bounding up the stairs to my bedroom, slamming my door on their cries of astonishment.

CHAPTER TWENTY-FIVE

I'm inside an MRI machine made of glass. Waves of water beat against the dome, which covers me. Grey, thrusting swirls of water and spray. I'm terrified the glass isn't strong enough to hold back this forceful tide. Each swell booms as it slams into the side of the dome. I know with certainty that if the water breaks through, I will have to swim for my life. The booming sound diminishes, replaced by a tapping. I close my eyes. I'm afraid to open them and see who is tapping on the glass dome. Tapping. I know it will be Coach tapping for me to join her in her seawater grave. Tapping. Tapping. Tapping.

I woke soaked in sweat. Under my quilt, I was still wearing the clothes I'd had on at dinnertime. The tapping sound filled my head. I squinted to see the numbers on my alarm clock. It was almost midnight. The tapping grew more insistent. It wasn't coming from my head at all. Someone was rapping on my bedroom window! My heart clenched. Who – aside from a ghost – could be knocking on my second-storey window? I summoned every ounce of courage left in me to meet Coach Nola again.

I flung my curtains back and saw an outstretched arm and a bare knuckle poised to knock. I had to press against the window to see the face looking at me from atop a ladder – the ladder Dad had been using to take down Christmas lights that week. Dodie Direland was looking at me through the cedar bush that grew up to my window. A mitten dangled between her clenched teeth. A toque sat low on her brow, almost covering the terrified look in her eyes. She shoved her bare-knuckled hand into the dangling mitten and grabbed the ladder rung. A stream of visible breath puffed out from between her lips.

I was so shocked to see her I panicked and yanked the curtain closed. A second later, I flung it open again, fearing that I'd caused her to fall off the ladder. I tugged hard on the window crank to make the frozen latch open.

"What are you doing here – up here?" I squeaked.

"Hi, Summer," she said, adjusting the woollen toque so she could see me better. "First, let me say that I'm not good with heights. Okay? Second, I'm glad they've stopped the practice of routine lobotomies. Third, it's freezing outside. Lastly, you have to get your butt out here and listen to me. Your Mom is at our house right now talking to my mom, and I overheard some stuff."

There was a point a few weeks earlier at which I thought I'd never speak to Dodie Direland again, but under the circumstances, what choice did I have? She was on a ladder, risking her life to tell me something. I whispered, "Wait at the side door of our garage. It's a little warmer in there. Be careful, Dodie. I'll be right down."

"Hurry," she insisted. "If your mom leaves and mine checks my room, I am so-o-o grounded." As she started down the ladder, I heard her mutter, "Actually, the ground part of that sounds pretty good."

I didn't wait to see if she reached the bottom. I realized that I might not be able to make it out of the house undetected myself. I shoved my parka on and very cautiously opened my bedroom door. No sign of anyone. I snuck down the hall, down the stairs. No one. I could see the basement light under the crack of the kitchen door. Dad must be down there. With any luck, he'd have his headphones on. I shoved my feet into the only pair of available sneakers and stole out the back door.

I could hear Dodie shivering before I spotted her in the dark. Leaning my shoulder against the garage door, I shoved hard. Dodie and I tumbled through it. I groped for the light switch.

"Are you all right?" I demanded.

"I was about to ask you the same question," Dodie replied.

"I'm okay, I guess."

There was an awkward silence, which Dodie eventually broke. "I was glad to hear your scan and everything checked out normal."

I nodded.

"So, did you freak out at dinner tonight?"

I half-shrugged.

Dodie looked at me and rubbed her woollen toque with her mittened hand. "Jeez, do MRIs decrease your verbal abilities, or what?"

I smirked. Dodie smirked back.

I said, "My parents want me to go back to school and to basketball."

"And?"

"Think about it, Dodie! Look, for a while, I blamed you for telling everyone about…about the ghost. I obviously can't stay mad at someone who climbs a ladder through a cedar bush for me. But I can't exactly go back to school, either, can I?"

"I don't think you have a choice, Summer. Well, actually, I overheard your mom telling mine that there were only two choices left. If you don't go back to school, she's considering a day-patient program for you at a mental health facility."

"What?" I had to reach for the garage wall to steady myself.

"She said until your violent outburst tonight, she would never have considered that course of action, but since you refuse to co-operate at optional therapy sessions, she doesn't know what else to do." Dodie paused before she went on. "I'm sorry. I shouldn't have been eavesdropping. I actually used a glass against the wall. That does work, surprisingly. I thought it was a scientific myth."

I cut Dodie off. "But I only flipped my dinner plate so that they wouldn't make me go back! Everyone at school is going to think I've lost my mind!"

"School's not so bad, Summer. Basketball sucks without you there. We haven't won a single game. I now have to play when the other girls are too tired. Coach Rogers yells at me the whole time so that even if I had any aptitude, I wouldn't be able to function out there." Dodie sighed. "Look, I still don't have the solution as to why you're being haunted, but I have done research on the brain. I believe I can explain the ghost away *medically* so that no one will think you're bonkers."

I huddled into my collar, ready to listen.

"I'm going to tell everyone at school that you had two brain scans. The first one showed an almost undetectable fluid mass resting midway between your parietal lobe and your occipital lobe. Your parietal lobe is the part of your brain that controls body senses, orientation, visual and spatial perception, while the occipital lobe controls vision. The tiny mass was pressing in on these two lobes, causing your visual perception to go wonky, making weird light appear, which looked remarkably like a ghost. I'll tell the girls on the team that because your vision went funny the night of the séance, you thought it was Coach Nola's ghost. Incidentally, I'll mention that the tiny fluid mass was probably a result of the blow to the head from the basketball they hit you with that night. That should make them feel guilty enough to be nice for a while. Anyway, then I'll tell them that your second scan showed that the tiny mass had all but disappeared and you aren't experiencing visual or perception problems any longer. Voila! Cured!"

"But my mom will tell the school there's nothing wrong with my brain," I insisted.

"I heard your mom tell mine that she already reported to the school that there's been no conclusive diagnosis at this point, but the doctors recommend you start attending classes again. You know how rumours fly around the school? In the end, no one will trace my story back to me, and if they do, I'll just say I overheard some teachers talking and I thought they were referring to you. Simple. Just stay home one more day, and I'll have the entire school convinced by the time you arrive the following morning. Deal?"

I hesitated. "Do you really think my mom would put me in some kind of facility if I don't return to classes?"

Dodie looked at the ground. As if this prompted her to remember how cold her feet were, she started to stomp in an attempt to warm them and restart her circulation. She didn't look up when she finally answered. "If she spends any more time under my mom's influence, she'll have you committed."

"So it was your mom's idea?" I blurted out accusingly.

"Afraid so" was all Dodie could muster. She glanced at me then with an abject look of apology.

I asked, "So that's really why you climbed the ladder and invented this elaborate lie on my behalf?"

Dodie nodded. She bit her lip.

The silence stretched into awkwardness until I finally sighed and said, "Okay, so if anyone asks, I say I had fluid pressing on some lobes in my brain, which caused me to see things that weren't really there. But I'm okay now, right?"

Dodie beamed at me. "Right, and remind them to wear a helmet when they do extreme sports or ride their bikes. Act like a poster girl for brain injuries."

"Dodie!"

"Okay, well, only if you feel comfortable with that. I mean it is a good idea to wear a helmet even if you look like a geek, right?"

I shook my head at her. "You'd better get yourself one before you decide to climb any more ladders."

Laughter bubbled between us. Dodie suddenly hugged me. "Everything will be fine, Summer. I'm glad you're okay."

I was overwhelmed by Dodie's hug. "Thanks," I managed to mutter. "I hope I really am okay." I paused. "I've still seen a ghost, haven't I? Doesn't that scare you, Dodie, especially considering, in reality, there appears to be nothing wrong with my brain?"

"Worst-case scenario," Dodie said, pulling off her mitten and tapping her fingers into her palm. "Coach Nola really is a ghost. I was never afraid of Coach Nola; why should I be afraid of her ghost? Now, Coach Rogers, that's a different matter. That guy is truly scary."

I shook my head. "Why are you afraid of Coach Rogers? If he has to pick on teenage girls to feel good about himself, then we should pity him, not fear him."

"Well, for one thing," Dodie continued, counting things on her fingers, "I'm afraid that he'll get so mad at me that he'll have a heart attack and come back as a ghost. Who is he going to haunt? You're looking at her!"

I chuckled.

She raised a second finger. "More importantly, he could tell me to go home and not come back. And that is what I'm most afraid of…not having a hope of ever playing this game again. You're lucky, Summer. You're a natural athlete. Those of us who aren't are always afraid of being tossed aside – so afraid, that most of us don't bother to come back of our own accord. Once we're cut, we're gone. We throw in the towel, take up scrapbooking. Your fears, Summer, are free to run elsewhere."

"Yeah, like to apparitions? Dodie, it's all perspective, you know?"

Dodie looked at me hard then, under the bare garage light bulb.

I jumped in. "The story goes that Michael Jordan was cut from his high school team, Dodie, and look what happened!"

She considered that for a moment. "Maybe you're right, Summer," she said, and pushed her hand back into her mitten. "Now you're starting to sound like me – that might be your biggest worry yet!"

I laughed at her, and she smiled.

"Anyway," she continued, "Coach Rogers says that if we can start a winning streak, we still have a chance at a wild card into the Provincials. We're too far down the rankings now to do it any other way. If you come back, Summer, we still have a shot at it. The team needs you. Everybody on the team knows that without a doubt now. And it's what she wanted, right?" Dodie stamped her feet again. The garage was still freezing.

"I know that's what she wanted back then. I don't know what she wants now," I said quietly, and I watched the icy fog of my breath for a brief second before it disappeared. I shivered.

"Look, Summer, let's have a signal if she shows again, so that you don't have to deal with it by yourself, okay? Pull your jersey out of your shorts if she shows, then tuck it back in, and I'll focus my energy on trying to see her or intercepting a message or something."

I shook Dodie's mittened hand. We had a deal.

CHAPTER TWENTY-SIX

Garvin Invaders	Opposing Team
29	32
36	34
44	38
39	37
35	28
41	27

Those were the scores of our next six games. Five straight wins after a close loss. In each game, I had scored at least half the points. I seemed to have come back a stronger player. I didn't know if it was the training session with Everett and Baxter at the university or if it was the three-week rest. Coach Rogers expected me to be out of shape and was treating me with kid gloves, but I was actually bursting with energy. Part of that energy must have been pure relief. Sometimes the things you worry about the most are the things that turn out to be the least of your worries. Dodie had done a bang-up job of damage control at school. Everyone seemed to believe her story, and apart from catching up on my school work, it was as if I hadn't been away at all. The one exception was when my teammates swarmed me at my first practice in an unexpected group hug.

Dodie had her own theory about my supercharged energy. Through careful observation during those six games, she speculated that the energy trace of Coach was actually quite powerful and that maybe it was actually channelling through me.

"Dodie," I said. "First you don't believe in ghosts, and now you think the ghost is giving me super powers?"

"I know it sounds strange, Summer, but each time you've pulled out your jersey, it's immediately after you've made four or five spectacular plays in a row – the kind where you drive end to end and score. I look around, and apart from the weird scoreboard thing, there are always a few student spectators who pull out their earbuds or start twiddling with their iPods as if something odd has just happened – dead battery or volume change. There's definitely an energy disturbance, Summer. Even though I can't see her, I know for certain there is something out there."

"Wow," I muttered, convinced for the first time that I wasn't losing my mind after all. "Then maybe she is coming because she wants us to win."

"Maybe," Dodie answered, and the look of excitement on her face made my stomach stir.

Maybe we were going to win the Provincials! The Garvin underdogs were going to kick some provincial basketball butt!

By the time we were ready to play our final league game – the one that would decide whether we were eligible for the provincial wild card seed in the playdowns – I was beginning to anticipate, not dread, Coach Nola's appearances on the court. Bring on the power! Dodie and I huddled in the corner before the game started, and although Karmyn and Roxx exchanged looks with each other, they weren't hassling Dodie or me. We were finally all focused on the win.

"So, Dodie, I'm going to leave a corner of my jersey untucked if she's sticking around, okay? I'll try and point out her general direction and make it look like it's part of the play or something. Keep making your observations as long as you see the jersey untucked."

Dodie nodded and said, "Remember how she called you our Secret Weapon at that final practice?"

I nodded.

"It's ironic, but now you really are." Dodie grinned.

"More like *she's* our Secret Weapon," I said, and we high-fived.

The whistle blew to start the game. I could hear Dodie's mom cheering and I caught sight of my parents at courtside. By the half, we were five points up on Nostrum School.

"Listen up girls," Coach Rogers said in the break. "I want you to start the half strong. If we can score another three or four unanswered baskets right off the top of the half, then I think this game is in the bag. Strictly maintenance after that! Go out there, look for the open lane, pressure for the interception, don't give up the ball, got it? One, two, three..."

"Invaders!"

I thought that was my cue. Coach Rogers wanted us to crank the thermostat to high.

Karmyn, Roxx, Faith, Trish and I took to the court. I intercepted the throw-in and sent it right into Roxx's hands. She passed to Karmyn, who struggled to beat her check. I broke open and called for the ball. Karmyn continued to drive. Her check stayed on her until she was too far under the basket to get a proper shot off. Nostrum grabbed the rebound, and with a quick break, they scored, narrowing our lead to three.

I ran over to Karmyn. "Pass the ball next time," I spat out, furious. "I was wide open!"

Karmyn wouldn't meet my eyes, but my parents tried to catch mine, and when I glanced over, their eyebrows were raised. They didn't understand what was at stake. Provincials or bust!

In the next play, Faith went down hard and skinned her knee. She limped off the court bleeding, and my heart sank. We needed her. Tracy was subbed in, but she had two turnovers in a row and Nostrum tied the game. Coach Rogers called a time out. Dodie had Faith's knee bandaged by that time, but she was still limping. Coach Rogers told her to ice it for a few minutes so she could play the final portion of the game. He subbed Dodie in, and I felt the tension among the players rise. Dodie turned pale. From the looks on the other players' faces, Dodie hadn't improved in the time I'd been away. Why wasn't CJ being subbed in? Even Val was a better option, though she had a bad cold.

Coach Rogers said, "Summer, you get inside. Girls, get the ball in to Summer down low. Execute!"

The ref blew his whistle and I caught a whiff of coconuts. I turned and saw her at half-court. I yanked my jersey out and just as Roxx passed the ball to Dodie, Dodie took note of my jersey. She glanced at the scoreboard and scanned the bleachers. Nostrum intercepted the ball, ran right past Nola Blythe and scored.

Coach Rogers yelled, "Direland, get your head in the game. Move to the pass!"

Dodie tried to refocus.

I ran past Dodie and yelled for Roxx to feed me the ball even though I was supposed to be headed down to Nostrum's key, waiting for the pass down low. Roxx passed to me in our end. I drove down the court, faked left and took the shot. Two points! A cheer rose from the Garvin fans. Coach Nola hovered at half-court. I knew the game was ours.

As we assumed our defensive positions, I whispered to Roxx and Karmyn. "Just don't give Dodie the ball, okay?" Then I sprinted over to Dodie and said, "Play hard defence. Don't sweat the rest."

She rallied with my words; she didn't even realize I was trying to keep her out of the play. I tried to convince myself she had a more important job to do, but I knew the reason I didn't want her near the ball was because we couldn't afford another turnover. I met Coach Nola's doleful expression and tried to convey telepathically that I knew she was there for us. Her blank eyes did nothing to reassure me. If she was there to feed me energy, why couldn't there be some lingering essence of the real live Nola Blythe rather than this vapid resemblance?

Dodie must have noticed my worried expression. The player she was supposed to be checking was advancing down the court, but Dodie was trying to signal something back to me. The player cut away from Dodie. Dodie didn't follow. The ball was in our hoop before I could do anything about it. Coach Rogers took Dodie off and put Tracy back in. Dodie looked relieved and continued to focus on centre court. I heard Coach Rogers swear at her under his breath. I was just happy she could concentrate on Coach Nola while I did what I had to do, and that was score some baskets to win the game. My jersey stayed out. After I scored three baskets in a row, Nostrum called a time out, and the ref came over and told me to tuck my jersey in. As soon as his back was turned, I pulled a side-piece out and pointed at it to show Dodie that Coach Nola was still there. I imagined Dodie could tell anyway: the score-board was dimming and pulsing. It flickered off, causing a short game delay that allowed me to catch my breath. When the scoreboard relit, it read Home 33, Guests 31.

I had to widen the margin, but when I drove in past the defence for a layup, the apparition suddenly appeared right in front of me. As the ball caromed off the backboard and out of my rebound reach, I stared at centre court. Coach Nola was no longer there; instead she was under the hoop with her vacant eyes. Nostrum scored and Coach Rogers called his final time out.

Reaching for my water bottle, I whispered to Dodie what had happened. "She doesn't seem to be on my side, Dodie," I said, shaking my head.

Dodie waited for me to tip back my water bottle, and then she said, "The disturbance is major tonight, Summer. I have a compass in my sports bag, and a moment ago it spun in circles. You've got to channel it, Summer. I know you can."

Coach Rogers yelled, "*Dire Straits*, stop interfering with Summer's concentration. I'm talking here and you're gossiping about some guy in the bleachers, no doubt. Did you hear the play, Summer?"

I looked embarrassed enough for him to repeat it, but it was Dodie's advice I was focused on. *Concentrate*, I told myself. *Channel the energy*.

We won the game. The final score was 45–39. The whole team celebrated at Little Italy Eatery with extra-large pizzas and pitchers of iced tea. We were going to the provincial playoffs!

The next morning, Dodie wasn't at school. I caught up with Val in the hallway.

"Hey Val, are you feeling any better? Did Dodie catch your bug?"

Val coughed into her hand and said, "Didn't you hear?"

"Hear what?" I asked, my heart turning to stone at the look on Val's face. Had Dodie seen the ghost too? Was she terrorized?

"Karmyn just told me that Coach Rogers phoned Dodie last night after we left the restaurant and told her he thought it would be best if she didn't suit up for the playoffs."

"What?" I exclaimed. "How does Karmyn know that?"

"Coach moved in with Karmyn's mom. Karmyn overheard him on the phone. He told Dodie she was welcome to stay on as team manager as long as she didn't talk to the players during the game."

"Why in the world would he do such a thing?" I cried out.

"According to Karmyn, he caught her playing with some electronic gadgets or something while she was on the bench. Plus, he said she nearly cost us the game with her screw-ups on the court, not to mention distracting you."

"But she wasn't distracting me."

"Well, the two of you were acting really odd during the game. Was there a boy in the stands or something?"

"No!" I exclaimed. "Why does everyone assume there's a boy as soon as someone is distracted?"

Val looked me straight in the eye and lowered her voice. “CJ says there’s something really odd about the two of you. She said her parents were driving her home from the mall one night and she saw you and Dodie down the street from Mel’s convenience store. You were wearing PJs and a parka, and the two of you were rolling in the snow. Together. She said it was too weird!”

“What?” I shook my head in disbelief. “What has any of that got to do with Dodie being kicked off the team?” I demanded.

Val answered by adding, “CJ says that maybe the real reason you were away from school for so long is that your parents were trying to keep the two of you apart.”

I narrowed my eyes at Val and shook my head. It was pointless talking to her. She had been sucked in by the others. She probably felt safer being part of their posse than being a target. That I could understand.

“Maybe,” I ventured, “CJ should spend more time worrying about her basketball skills than starting stupid rumours. Dodie was subbed in before her last night.”

Val just sighed and said, “That’s because CJ finally started her monthlies yesterday and didn’t want to play. If you cared about anyone else on the team, Summer, you would have known that.”

“Well,” I said, as I stomped away. “Now that Dodie is kicked off the team, CJ will have to play regardless, won’t she?” Under my breath, I muttered, “Try playing basketball when you have your period *and* a ghost!”

CHAPTER TWENTY-SEVEN

I stewed about everything Val had said to me for most of the day and fell further behind on my school work. My notes were blank, my assignments unfinished. The reason I couldn't concentrate was due to my feelings of guilt over Dodie being cut from the team. It was my fault that Dodie had been so distracted the night before. She was trying to gather ghost data for me when she should have been concentrating on the game. And, even though I felt guilty, I also saw the benefit in Dodie's removal. If she didn't have to worry about playing, she could do ghost patrol that much more effectively. Thinking such selfish thoughts pricked my conscience until it itched. I knew in my heart that I supported not letting Dodie back on the court. It was one thing for her to mess up a league game when we didn't have a chance at winning, but the provincial playoffs were looming, and at that level, Dodie wouldn't be able to contribute. She was more likely to prove detrimental to the team's success. Besides all of that, I was tired of people thinking I was weird. I didn't understand how anyone could consider that my rolling in the snow with Dodie could be weirder than my seeing apparitions, but if they did, maybe Coach Rogers' decision was for the best.

Before we started warm-up at that night's after-school practice, Coach Rogers called us into a meeting. He referred to his clipboard as if he had notes written there and didn't make eye contact with anyone. He rubbed the top of his forehead, the place that was usually reserved for smacking.

"Mrs. Direland was in touch with me this afternoon," he started. "And she has informed me that Dodie will not be attending any future games. Their decision follows a discussion I had with the family last night regarding Dodie's role on the team. They feel that it's not beneficial for Dodie to sit on the bench, so she's quitting." He cleared his throat and glanced around. "Any questions? If not, we have a lot of work to do girls, a lot of work if we have any hope of challenging the top provincial teams. And that's our job, so let's get to it. Let's start with five easy laps, then grab a ball and shoot ten free throws. Record your makes and misses. Let's go!"

For a moment I was too stunned to stand. He hadn't exactly lied, but he hadn't told the whole truth, either, had he? Dodie quitting? He was the one who told her she couldn't play on the team any longer. The girls didn't give his announcement a second thought; clearly, Karmyn had informed them already. They were on their third lap before I caught up to them.

Breathing hard, my nostrils were suddenly assaulted by the scent of coconut. It was so strong, I had to stop and cover my mouth and nose. I looked to centre court – nothing. I spun around and saw her sitting on the bench next to our gym bags and water bottles. I started a slow jog again and tried to stay on the inside of the other girls, but Coach Rogers yelled at me to stop cutting corners. Nola Bythe's eyes seemed to follow me, and even though I was sweating, my legs started to feel cold and heavy. I was slogging through a gym full of frigid waters. Why was she at practice, and why was she causing that mind-numbing cold? I picked up a ball and couldn't feel it in my fingers. Out of ten free throws, I made none.

"Zero? None? Nada?" Coach Rogers yelped when I told him my score. He smacked his head and looked to the other girls for more encouraging numbers.

"Eight!" Karmyn beamed.

"Good job! Your hard work is paying off, Karmyn. However, just because Direland isn't here any longer, doesn't mean we can't all work hard to match her free-throw stats, eh? Be nice to see some tens from the rest of you over the next week or two, and maybe fifty per cent from you, eh, *Withering Heights*?"

I nodded, embarrassed, grateful for the warmth that my blushing created. Dodie had ten out of ten on her free throw stats? I *had* missed something.

"Can we try ten again?" I called out to Coach Rogers.

He nodded. "Let's do that. Good suggestion, captain. Now, girls, that's leadership." He glanced over at Karmyn and added, "We have two very fine co-captains to lead this team to victory."

I felt my chest swell a little. He hadn't stressed my role as co-captain before. He tended to favour Karmyn at every turn until that moment. He'd made us equals.

I headed to the basket that was farthest from our bench to shoot my free throws. I settled my feet at the line, bent my knees, and adjusted my arms so that the ball was set high. I raised my eyes to look at my target. Coach Nola was right in front of the hoop. I stood and dribbled the ball away from the key for a moment, feeling my heart pound in my chest. *I will reset and shoot*, I told myself, *even if she's still there, and I will sink ten out of ten. I know that's what she wants me to do. I know that's why she's here.*

Out of ten throws, I sank zero again. Every one of them passed her and fell short, even though I thought I was throwing harder each time, and I concentrated on channelling her energy into me. My teeth started to chatter. I held my finger and thumb together to form a zero when Coach Rogers asked us our scores. He shook his head at me but said nothing. At least Karmyn's count fell to six. No one scored ten.

For the rest of the practice, there was no escaping her. She seemed to turn into my check, playing hard defence against me, forcing me into the corners, making me take the shot too quickly and off balance, forcing me to lose control of my dribble. At one point, I was so frustrated, I turned to the bench in tears. Why did Dodie believe that the ghost was there to super-charge me? She was sucking away my abilities instead. Dodie had said, "Channel it," at the last game, and I had. I scored three baskets in a row, and went to the foul line twice and shot four for four. We won because of me, or because of Nola Blythe's spirit through me. Or was it because Dodie had somehow managed to scientifically harness the energy? Did she have control of Coach Nola's spirit? And now that Dodie was off the team, would she reveal to her mother that I was still seeing the apparition? It had been a little too easy to convince my parents I was no longer being haunted. Dodie could wreak havoc if she wanted to get even.

Coach Rogers called for a water break and asked me if I was feeling okay. When I nodded and sniffled, he pointed to his smacking spot and asked, "You're not experiencing headaches, dizziness, spots in front of your eyes?" I knew that was his polite way of asking if I was seeing things.

"I'm okay," I told him. When I reached for my water bottle, I was staring into Coach Nola's hollow eyes, and my heart started pounding so hard that it was knocking the breath right out of my lungs. My eyes darted around the room. None of the other girls looked as if they were lacking oxygen, despite the hard practice. At that precise moment, the gym lights dimmed. The hollow empty feeling I'd experienced on Christmas Eve came rushing back. For a moment, I felt as if I was falling from a great height. As if I was about to crash.

Everyone was commenting on the lights dimming when I shouted, "Wait!" The lights surged back to normal.

Coach Rogers, who was walking away to talk to the twins, stopped abruptly. Everyone turned their attention from the lights and their water bottles to me.

"I'm not fine!" I said. "I'm not fine with the decision to cut Dodie from this team!" I needed Dodie. I was terrified that Coach Nola was going to follow me home and stay with me forever!

Coach Rogers cleared his throat. "Well, Dodie was welcome to remain a part of this team," he muttered. "I just couldn't guarantee her any court time as we head into these playoffs. It was her choice not to come back."

I didn't know how to proceed, but it was too late to turn back. Karmyn was smirking. CJ's mouth was hanging open as if she couldn't believe what she was hearing. Val was focused on the floor to avoid looking at me. I realized I was much more afraid of the ghost's melancholy eyes than of my teammates.

I kneaded my brain, forcing it to find the right words. "Dodie isn't the best player," I finally said. "We all know that, but she's the most positive influence on this team. She never gets down even though her role is plank-riding, bench-warming – whatever. If Dodie isn't brought back, then I quit!" I threw my water bottle into my bag and headed for the change room.

There were audible gasps behind me. Coach Rogers swallowed hard before he cleared his throat and said, "Okay, girls, okay, just do a couple of cool-down laps. We'll call it a day. Make sure you stretch it out." His voice dwindled as if he wasn't sure what his own words meant.

I turned back and flung a final sentence. "She deserves to wear the uniform as much as any of us!"

No one followed me into the change room. After I dressed and opened the door, I saw the team sitting on the bleachers in discussion with Coach Rogers. I ran out of the gym, taking one quick glimpse behind to see if Coach Nola was following me. There was no sign of her, but I nearly tripped over Mr. Portney's wheeled mop bucket in the hallway.

"Watch where you're going!" he called out before he saw it was me. His face turned a dull crimson when I turned around and gave him the one-finger salute.

I called out, "If you go squealing to Principal Talbot that I did that, I'll convince my shrink to get a restraining order against you."

Mr. Portney's reddened face registered alarm. A shock of power rippled through me followed by a wave of shame. I had to be in control of one thing in my life, even if it was Mr. Portney. Was I going to threaten everyone I knew with rash behaviour? Maybe I could tell my parents that if they put me in a day program, I'd run away from home. I could threaten that I'd run so far, they'd never see me again as long as they lived. I wondered if Coach Nola could find me then. Maybe ghosts don't follow you when you hit rock-bottom.

CHAPTER TWENTY-EIGHT

"You see, Summer…" Mom was talking from the front passenger seat and I wanted her to stop, but it had been so long since I'd heard her punctuate her sentences with laughter that I tried to listen despite the sick feeling in my stomach. We were driving into Winnipeg for the Grade Eight Provincial Basketball Final against the Westun Junior High Wolverines, and it was as if my central nervous system was hooked into the car alternator and charging. Outside, the streets were slushy from the March thaw, and the last sinking sun rays were burning my eyes.

Mom prattled on. "…When I heard how you stuck up for Dodie and had her reinstated on the team, I was so proud of you. Martha told me how much that meant to Dodie. I think the goodwill you exhibited has come back to you as good fortune, and here you are on the cusp of something amazing!"

I mumbled an acknowledgement, knowing that it was desperation – not goodwill – that caused me to threaten to quit the team if Dodie wasn't brought back.

Dad glanced in the rear-view mirror at me. "No matter what the outcome of tonight's game, you've been a true leader on the team."

Mom didn't wait for my response. "Imagine little Garvin versus the basketball mammoths at Westun. Some of those girls have been playing basketball since they were five years old."

"Who told you that?" I asked.

"Mrs. Direland Googled them. Their sports department

has their own webpage and there are profiles of the girls that you can click on. You should talk to Coach Rogers about that for the Invaders for next year."

There won't be a next year, I thought. I'm not sharing the basketball court with a ghost for another year. Coach Nola's existence during the quarter- and semi-final playoffs had been almost too much to bear. Dodie had been allowed to keep a stats clipboard with special statistics for me that Coach Rogers allowed us to discuss privately during time outs. He didn't ask any questions, and although I could tell the other girls were dying to know what the sheets said, they seemed to have been warned to stay away. How could we have explained them? Stat #1: CN's ghost interferes with the play right after a three-basket or more Summer-run. Stat #2: When S calls for subs, CN disappears. Stat #3: Whenever S goes to the line for a foul shot, CN hovers above the hoop. Dodie and I had required a more complex signal system to try to determine why Coach Nola was no longer simply present but a part of every game. If it had not been for Dodie's constant assurances that with enough gathered data the apparition's appearance was a decipherable mystery, I would never have finished the season.

When we arrived at the Wolverines' gymnasium, loud rap music was pumping from the speakers. One side of the gym was a sea of red t-shirts and banners for the Wolverines home team. Our side of the gym was beginning to fill as well. Principal Talbot had arranged for a school bus to transport our student fans from Garvin into the city. My parents, Holly, Everett and even Baxter were in the crowd. We had never played in front of so many people before, and a shiver ran through me. As we left our bags and water bottles at our bench to prepare for warm-up, I turned to Dodie and whispered, "Tell me again why you think she interferes when I'm doing well – like after I've scored a few baskets?"

Dodie was peeling off her warm-up shirt. Upon my insistence, Coach Rogers had agreed to let Dodie dress for each game with her name on the roster even though she never came off the bench and had been relegated, once again, to shooting free throws on her own during most of our practices. She had assured me she was fine with that.

"Well, Summer," she stated. "I think that after you've scored a few unanswered baskets, she senses that you're tired or that you start to relax too much, so she's challenging you to continue strong, to continue working hard."

I grimaced. "That's kinda backwards thinking, Dodie. I'm already tired; I don't need two checks on me. A real one and her."

"She's see-through, Summer," she reminded me with a droll expression. "And you can run right through her without drawing a personal foul."

I laughed. Dodie could be funny even in that pressure-cooker atmosphere.

"Besides," Dodie added "lots of athletes have to play in spite of their coaches and not because of them."

The two-minute buzzer sounded. The music was switched off and Coach Rogers hailed us in for a huddle. All he said was "Go do this, girls!" Then he turned it over to the captains.

Karmyn added, "Let's destroy them." She looked at me to see if I had anything to add.

I glanced at Coach Rogers. It was the Provincial Final, and he couldn't exactly bench me, so I risked it. "Girls, think back to the start of this season, when this team took a major blow."

Dodie's head swivelled, and she looked at me questioningly as if she wasn't sure I should continue.

I pressed on. "The last night Coach Nola was with our team, she recited a quote she wanted me to memorize. She said, 'It's not whether you win or lose, it's how you win the game.'"

The girls looked at each other, puzzled.

Karmyn spoke up. "That's not how the saying goes," she declared.

"I know. It was Coach Nola's twist on the expression."

CJ piped in, "What the heck is it supposed to mean, Summer?"

"It means that we *have* to win. There's no place for *losing* in her philosophy…it's how you *win* the game. You do whatever it takes. So let's go *win* for Coach Nola!"

The girls rallied. "Yeah! Invaders!" they yelled. All except Dodie. She was busy scribbling something on the stats clipboard.

The buzzer sounded. Dodie tried to catch my eye, but the emcee started introducing the team players. When they called my name and a cheer rose from our side of the bleachers, I blushed and stared at the floor.

A few moments later, I won the jump ball to start the game. Within seconds of that, we had our first turnover, and before we could even put a shot up in the Wolverines zone, they had jumped to a six-point lead. The sea of red was cheering as if they'd already won the championship. Coach Rogers called a time out. Coach Nola hadn't yet shown; maybe she wasn't coming. Maybe making it to the Provincial Final had been her goal, and now that we had reached it, she was gone. Dodie pulled me aside as soon as I came off the court.

"Summer, did you mean what you said, or was that just rallying the team spirit? No pun intended!"

"What?" I asked, confused.

"Did you mean that Coach's statement had no room for losing? Is that how you interpreted what she'd said to you?"

"Well, yeah," I replied. "How else could you interpret it?"

The ref blew his whistle and was holding the ball on the sideline, waiting for our throw-in. I had to get back on the court.

Dodie yanked me back by the jersey and said, "I'm sure that's not what she meant, Summer. I don't believe she was a win-at-all-costs coach or she would never have wasted her time encouraging players like me."

I frowned at Dodie and pushed her hand off my jersey. My jersey was yanked out as she released it. The ref pointed and told me to tuck it back in.

Dodie called after me, "Think about it, Summer. She meant something else."

Could Dodie be right? Had I misinterpreted Coach Nola's statement all this time? I shook my head at Dodie in disbelief, and a second later, coconut scent surrounded me. I clawed at my jersey before she even appeared.

The ref walked over to me, glared, and said, "I thought I just told you to tuck that in."

"Sorry," I said, and attempted to leave an inconspicuous corner untucked.

The Wolverines stormed down the court with two more baskets to make it 10–0 before Coach Nola materialised. The home crowd was stomping on the bleachers, delighted with their team's dominance. I heard Coach Rogers yelling at me to get my head in the game; my head was so confused.

"What do you want?" I yelled at the apparition and dared those blank eyes to wake up and see me. "What?" I heard myself demand again.

Coach Rogers thought I was talking to him. "Give and go," he yelled. "Get some points up on the board."

The "give and go" meant he wanted me to feed Karmyn to score. She would pass to me and cut to the key, and then I would pass it back before her check could defend.

When Karmyn passed it in, I turned to the hoop myself and shot from the outside. I scored. Cheers and whistles rose from the Garvin bleachers.

"The play was give and go!" Karmyn raged at me as we reassembled in our defensive end.

"I had the open shot, I took it," I insisted.

The next play, Karmyn tried to drive in to the hoop on her own, but her check was quicker than she was, and she couldn't penetrate. Her check knocked the dribble free; I lunged for the ball, grabbed it and drove hard for the layup. I scored again.

The Wolverines' coach screamed, "Who's on number

seven? Don't make her look good!"

I knew the defence would tighten on me, so the next play, I passed over to Faith and she dropped another one in. Her check had been trying to cheat over in my direction in case I drove in again, leaving Faith open. The Wolverines' coach threw down his clipboard and called a time out. It was pretty early in the game for that much coach anger. Our team ran in toward the bench with smiles on our faces even though we were still losing by four points.

"She's here?" Dodie whispered.

"Yeah, but she's hanging way back in the corner right now," I said.

"Summer," Dodie said, "do you want her to stay there? Away from the play?"

I nodded.

"Then do the give and go."

"But Karmyn's check is too fast. It won't work," I said.

"Just try it," Dodie said. "I'm testing a new theory. After the play, point her direction out to me."

The give and go resulted in a turnover, and although Coach Nola stayed put, the Wolverines scored.

I pointed and glared back to the bench at Dodie, but she scribbled something on the clipboard and ignored me. There were no more coaching tips from her, so I poured on the energy and scored another three unanswered baskets. When I turned to look at the bench, Coach Nola was hovering in between. I looked away and grew more determined.

Maybe Nola Blythe's spirit was feeding off my energy rather than the other way around. Maybe that was the new theory Dodie was testing. Maybe the energy I was generating was what fed her; in turn, she transformed the energy into some kind of electrical disturbance. If we hadn't held the séance and created that circle of joined-hand team energy, maybe she would never have been able to come back. I pointed to mid-court to show Dodie that she had moved in. Dodie scribbled furiously.

I was determined for the rest of the half to generate more and more energy on my own so that Coach Nola's spirit could be part of this Provincial Final. At the half, we were leading by four points. Our comeback had subdued the Wolverine bleachers as we headed into the halftime. As the Wolverines' school band struck up the theme from *Rocky*, I wasn't certain how I could possibly sustain a second half. My body was exhausted, and Coach Nola was so close to me on the court that I was afraid I would breathe her vaporous self right into me. I instinctively kept my mouth closed and breathed hard through my nose, which didn't allow for maximum oxygen flow. I flopped down on the floor beside our bench and buried my sweaty face in my towel. I could sense Dodie hovering over me in a worried state. The rest of the team did not come near us.

"Summer," she whispered. "Were you able to think about what I said while you were out there?"

I uncovered my eyes and glared at her.

She shook her head. "Okay, I know you were working your butt off with no time to think, but I believe that statement is somehow the key, Summer. You have to use it to unlock the reason behind her presence."

"Dodie," I said, "I can't think about all of this right now. This is the Provincial Final!"

"Okay," she nodded. "I understand." She wandered back to her spot on the bench, placed her clipboard upside down beside her and leaned her chin into her hands. She looked completely dejected. Our team was winning at the half, but Dodie looked as if we were beat.

Fury enveloped me. She really didn't care about the outcome of the game. She was only interested in whether her theory was correct or not. I wanted to yell at her, but I didn't have the strength to raise myself off the floor.

CHAPTER TWENTY-NINE

With two minutes left in the halftime, Dodie sidled over to where I was retying my shoes on the bench.

"Summer, I have to tell you something before you go back out there," she said, trying hard to hold my gaze. She signalled me to follow her away from the others. "This has been bothering me for a while."

I looked at her expectantly.

She took a deep breath. "I lied to you."

"About what?" I demanded and then lowered my voice. "What?" I repeated quietly. "Do you see her, too?"

"I lied to you about the compass and the electronic devices," she stated, not meeting my eyes. "There were no detectable power or magnetic disturbances. And all I had was a compass and a volt meter that wasn't hooked up to anything but air."

"But the scoreboard?" I said. "That didn't just happen in our gym, did it?" When she shrugged in response, I added, "Why in the world did you say those things?"

She answered, "Well, first off, I didn't want you believing you were losing your mind. When I told you that I couldn't see her but could detect an energy disturbance, you were better able to focus and didn't seem so worried. And when I said she must be channelling energy into you, your play really became super-charged! Plus, I thought we'd be better friends if I could share your burden with you and come up with a theory to make whatever it is you're going through bearable. I was trying to help, Summer."

"So you still doubt there's a ghost? You don't believe Coach Nola's spirit is here, do you?"

"I don't know what to think," Dodie said and glanced toward the scoreboard.

The clock was running down thirty seconds.

"But the scoreboard," I insisted.

She shrugged again. "It hasn't happened in this game yet," she finally blurted. "Different scoreboard." Then she quickly added, "I know that the only reason you demanded I be allowed back on this team was because you believed I was helping you with the ghost thing. I know I don't deserve to be here at the Provincial Final. I'm a complete spaz at basketball, so I just wanted to say I'm sorry I did that to you."

Dodie looked away and I could see tears brimming in her eyes. Dodie never cried, no matter how much she was bullied.

Guilt squeezed in my chest. "Hey," I said, struggling to think of something to say – something that wouldn't be a lie. "Hey, Coach Nola believed in you, remember? You played alongside the rest of us when she was our coach and she was always encouraging, remember?"

Dodie smiled feebly as the buzzer sounded, and she said, "Maybe the other reason I lied is that I wished I was the one who could see her," she mumbled.

She turned to sit on the bench as I headed for the throw-in to start the second half. We had possession, but I fumbled the pass. The Wolverines stole the ball and scored. Not an auspicious start to the half. I was still thinking about Dodie before I realized that Coach Nola wasn't on the court. She was hovering next to Dodie, so close that I was sure Dodie must feel her icy presence. Coach Rogers was yelling at me, but I couldn't really hear what he was saying over the roar of the Wolverines fans. They were chanting "Defence! Defence!" as Karmyn headed up the court with the ball. She passed to Roxx, who in turn attempted a shot herself rather than risk another turn-over by passing to me. She missed the shot, but I pulled the rebound out of the air, faded back and scored. I felt an inkling of relief as Roxx high-fived me.

As the second half progressed, the play became more and more critical. We were always within two baskets of each other. Sometimes we were winning, and sometimes the Wolverines inched ahead. Both teams were tightening their defence. More fouls were being called. Because we were going to the foul line more often, there were opportunities to catch my breath. I hadn't been subbed off yet in the second half. Coach Nola seemed to be allowing me some space to play. I tried to force her out of my mind. Dodie had me thinking again that the only place she existed was in my mind.

With two minutes remaining in the game, Karmyn fouled out. My heart sank. We were two points ahead, but as we headed in for the allowed time out and substitution, I knew we were in trouble. Tracy was going to have to carry the ball.

Coach Rogers attempted to focus Tracy on her task. "Protect the ball, Tracy! That's your job. Don't let them steal it. Make smart passes."

Tracy looked terrified as we headed to line up for the two foul shots. The Wolverines shooter missed both, and as I grabbed the rebound after the second shot, I didn't even look for Tracy. I drove down the court by myself and scored.

The Wolverines coach practically threw his chair onto the court. He was livid. Under two minutes and the score was 40–36. We were ahead by two baskets. The extra basket gave me some confidence that we could hold them off even without Karmyn if I could just dig deep. The Wolverines coach screamed for a time out. One minute and thirty seconds on the clock. Dodie didn't talk to me in the break. Coach Nola hovered at the edge of the court. I told myself that she wasn't really there.

The Wolverines used a pick and roll on Tracy three times in a row. We couldn't penetrate their defence to answer. We became frantic and scrambled. They had pulled ahead by two points. Coach Rogers hollered for time out with fifteen seconds on the clock and a roof about to rise off its moorings from the crowd chanting and stomping the bleachers.

He had to yell to be heard. "Summer, take the ball up the court. You'll have to score and then we press them hard so they can't get back. Win this now! At least tie the game, and we'll win it in overtime."

My heart was thudding in my chest. Tracy passed the ball to me under our own basket, and I started up the court. My check was tight on me as soon as I crossed centre. As I made an attempt to fake left on her, she anticipated and stole the ball right from underneath me. I pounded down the court after her and just as she put the shot up, I jumped to block it. It was all ball. A clean block that knocked the ball out of bounds. The crowd roared on both sides. The Wolverines coach jumped up and down, yelling, "Foul!" The ref held up his arm in the direction of the coach, trying to settle him down. Their coach snapped his clipboard in half over his knee and threw both halves onto the court. The ref blew his whistle and made the T sign with his hands, pointing at the Wolverines bench. Technical foul to the Wolverines coach with six seconds remaining on the clock. The Wolverines fans were on their feet in wild protest.

Coach Rogers called his final time out. I turned toward the bench, but Coach Nola hovered between me and it. I was suddenly immobilized. I bent down and put my hands on my knees as if I was trying to catch my breath. The coconut smell burned my nostrils. Blood was pounding so hard behind my eyes that it seemed the very gymnasium was pulsing. Nola Blythe's quote started looping in my brain. *It's not whether you win or lose – it's how you win the game. How? How* you *win* the game. Then clarity struck! I understood. You *win* as a team. You *win* with your best effort and your best self. I knew what I had to do. I lurched to the bench.

Coach Rogers stared at me. "Summer, are you all right?"

I shook my head, no.

"Summer, you have to take these foul shots. Take some deep breaths. Relax," he insisted.

I shook my head again. "No, I'm not taking them," I said.

Coach Rogers tossed his clipboard onto the bench. "Summer, Karmyn is fouled out. You *have* to take these shots."

"No," I refused. "Dodie has to take these shots."

Dodie jumped off the bench. "No way!" she exclaimed.

The team looked at me as if I had completely lost my mind.

"Coach Rogers," I said, my voice steady as I stared him in the eye, "Dodie has the best free-throw percentages on this team. That's all she's been allowed to practise since you took over coaching. Put her in. I'm the captain, and I'm not taking those shots."

"Summer," Dodie pleaded.

I turned to her. "You can do this, Dodie, better than any of us. I shot zero for twenty at a recent practice. We need these points to tie the game. You're the one, Dodie."

Coach Rogers smacked his head and looked bewildered.

Karmyn took a deep breath and stepped forward. "Let Dodie take the shots, Coach," she said, glancing up at me and then back down at the floor. "Summer is right. Dodie is the best choice."

I nodded at Karmyn and looked around at my teammates.

"Are you sure?" he asked us both. The ref blew his whistle. All the girls were nodding.

Val patted Dodie on the back. "You can do this, Dodie!" Everyone agreed.

Coach Rogers gave Dodie a dubious thumbs-up and called for substitution. Tracy stayed behind as Dodie made her way onto the court for the first time in the Provincials.

I walked beside her, my hand on her shoulder. "You were right, Dodie. I know now. Coach Nola wanted us, and me as captain, to learn *how* to win. The right way – as a team – with the proper attitude and spirit. I wish I'd figured that out before this game. Coach Nola believed in you, Dodie. You *can* do this. I know it. Absolutely."

A complete hush descended over the Wolverines gymnasium as Dodie Direland took her place at the foul line. The rest of us from both teams were lined up at half-court, not allowed at the key because the foul was a technical. I glanced over and saw Dodie's mom sitting with her eyes covered. My mom had her crossed fingers pressed to her lips as if she was kissing them for good luck, and Dad was nodding his head in approval. Holly, Everett and Baxter held a sign up high in the air and pointed at it: *My sister is number seven*, but I could barely read it.

Dodie spun the ball in her hands once and bounced it once. Her little ritual. The first shot swished and the Garvin stands erupted. Principal Talbot could be heard cheering above the rest of the crowd. I wanted to run in and high-five her, but I had to stay put at half-court. The ref bounced the ball back to Dodie and held his finger in the air to indicate one shot remaining. A second hush fell on the crowd. The scoreboard displayed 42–41 for the Wolverines. Dodie was shooting for the tie.

She glanced over her shoulder at me and I pointed to under the hoop. Coach Nola was pulsating there. I nodded encouragement to Dodie. She spun the ball once and bounced it once and then she put the ball up. On release, it looked perfect. But the ball struck the back of the hoop and bounced to the front, and with a quick lick of the rim, it spun out. I couldn't believe my eyes! How could she have missed? I'd been so certain. A swell of panic rose up inside me. There were only six seconds remaining on the clock. It was our possession at half-court, and I knew the throw-in was coming to me. CJ took it at the sideline and snapped the ball out to me. Immediately I was double-teamed. The two players swarming me waved their arms and swatted at the ball. I couldn't risk putting the ball down to dribble, and though I tried to pivot, I had no space. Our only open player was Dodie. She was still standing at the free throw line, terrified to be part of the play.

I had no choice. I stayed low and bounce-passed the ball to her, hoping I could free up for the give and go. Dodie caught the ball and clutched it to her chest, but the two Wolverine players stayed with me instead of following the ball. I tried, but couldn't break out. The Provincial Championship was falling away from us as the seconds skimmed off the clock. We would lose by one point. One point! Dodie's eyes were frantic, willing me to get free for the pass. CJ called for the ball on the other side of her, but Dodie would not take her eyes off me.

I shrieked with every last ounce of energy left in me. "Shoot, Dodie, shoot!"

Dodie pivoted, eyed the hoop and released the ball. It swished through the net. Astonished cries erupted from both sides of the gymnasium. The ref's hand shot sideways with his two fingers pointed at the ground – two points! The Wolverines coach bellowed for a time out, but had none remaining. As the Wolverines scrambled to receive the pass from under our basket, the buzzer sounded to end the game.

We swarmed Dodie. Our bench emptied, piling onto us at the foul line, where Dodie stood in shock. We screamed with joy, jumped around her, slapped her on the back, patted her head.

Finally she looked at me and screamed, "We won! We won!"

"You did it, Dodie," I screamed back at her. "*You* won the game!"

Dodie scanned for her mom in the bleachers. Mrs. Direland was sobbing in my parents' arms. Holly, Everett and Baxter were waving and hooting hoorays in our direction!

I pointed at the scoreboard.

Dodie looked up, but I knew I was still the only one who could see the spirit. For a split second, Coach Nola's eyes met mine as if she could finally see me. There was a flicker of approval, and then – as if someone threw a switch – Coach Nola Blythe vanished.

EPILOGUE

Principal Talbot held a special school assembly in our team's honour. Dodie received the Most Improved Player Award from Coach Rogers, and I was named the MVP. We both received bursaries to attend the Herdsmen's Spring Break Basketball Camp at the university. At that same assembly, Principal Talbot announced he was pleased to report that the manufacturer's defect of the scoreboards in our school division would be corrected shortly. He gave a special thanks to Mr. Portney for looking into the faulty products and assured us that our own scoreboard would be repaired in plenty of time for the next basketball season of the Garvin Invaders.

ACKNOWLEDGEMENTS

My gratitude extends to the entire Coteau team for their support and expertise, and to my editor, Kathryn Cole, for coaching me through the process with her keen observations.

For their rounds of encouragement, inspiration or critique, I want to thank Sheila McClarty, Sharon Caseburg, Kim Boughton, members of the Selkirk Literary Guild, my husband, David, and my children, Phil and Miranda. I am a big fan of all of you!

I also wish to remember Wayne, Tom and Tara, whose positive influences resonate here.

ABOUT THE AUTHOR

PATTI GRAYSON has written two adult works, *Core Samples* and *Autumn, One Spring*, which have garnered several Manitoba Book Award nominations. Her second book was also recently translated and released in Germany.

She attended both Western University in London, Ontario and the University of Winnipeg, and since then has enjoyed a varied career path. Patti has performed in film, radio and television, written ad copy, toured as a puppeteer and worked as a school librarian. As a youth, she loved playing sports, and has subsequently spent countless hours sitting on gym bleachers watching her own children compete.

Parts of *Ghost Most Foul* were written in the wilds of Northwestern Ontario, but Patti spends the majority of her year residing near Winnipeg, Manitoba.